M000291426

ANOTHER VERSION OF TRUTH

Palmetto Publishing Group
Charleston, SC

Another Version of Truth
Copyright © 2020 by Missy Lane
All rights reserved

No portion of this book may be reproduced, stored in a retrieval system, or transmitted
in any form by any means–electronic, mechanical, photocopy, recording, or other
except for brief quotations in printed reviews, without prior permission of the author.

First Edition

Printed in the United States

ISBN-13: 978-1-64111-719-7
ISBN-10: 1-64111-719-2

ANOTHER VERSION
OF TRUTH

MISSY LANE

CHAPTER ONE

Randi had to restrain herself from bounding out of the lawyer's office two stairs at a time. This was certainly no time for a turned ankle. It had taken much longer than she'd planned, but she was finally the owner of Willow Bend, or at least what remained of it.

She'd prevailed against the other bidders, fulfilling a vow she'd made so many years ago. It had literally been a lifetime since she'd left her home in South Carolina. She'd scarcely been seven years old when her mother uprooted her for parts unknown.

Randi took a deep breath as she once again considered the enormity of her actions. Today she'd closed the real estate deal that would reunite her with her beloved childhood home. Today she would use the key she'd been given to swing the gates open, and tonight she would once again rest her head at Willow Bend.

She was taking on quite a project as the property had been used as a hunting club since the 1970s. Her mother had sold almost everything even before her father was declared dead, and the new owner had promptly leased it to a group of hunters. As far as the attorney knew, there had been no permanent residents at Willow Bend during that time. In the years Randi had been gone, game plots had replaced rows of cotton, and sportsmen had poured in by the hundreds to take advantage of the native populations of turkey, deer and wild hogs. The area boasted some of the finest hunting in the world, and land leases had allowed many families to prosper despite rising property taxes and fluctuating crop prices.

The owner's heirs had recently divided Willow Bend into smaller tracts to maximize the profit opportunity, and that had been a big break for Randi. Land values had increased tenfold since the sixties, and she wouldn't have been able to assemble the resources to buy it in its entirety. It had been a little over seven thousand acres back then, but the three hundred she'd just purchased were all that mattered to her. The house and outbuildings were clustered on a parcel situated at the end of a half-mile lane that meandered through a mixed forest of long leaf pine and hardwoods. The lawyer maintained that it hadn't been logged in at least 30 years, so the value of the timber had naturally been a factor when determining what would be an acceptable bid.

Randi got in her truck and headed out of town, eager to close the fifteen-mile gap that separated her from her prize. She couldn't believe she was finally going home, and her heart pounded in her chest as she drove. Her excitement was replaced by more of a nervous anxiety the closer she got. She'd bought the place sight unseen despite the lawyer's stern warning that the house was in disrepair. She'd tried to prepare herself for the possibility that the house would be past saving, but it was a thought she dared not contemplate. She was a widow with dwindling resources, and she didn't exactly have a Plan B. Since Bill's death, Randi had been on a singular mission to return to the only home she'd ever known until the time her mother had packed their things with little warning and even less apology.

She wondered now what Bill would think of what she'd done. Would he approve of her ditching the life they'd made? She'd quit a great teaching job and sold their house. She'd said farewell to friends, Bill's parents, and a dear sister-in-law. She'd told them she needed a clean break and a fresh start, and they seemed to understand. As she got closer to her destination, she wondered if she wasn't just trading one set of bad memories for another. Watching Bill die had been gut-wrenching, and their friends and his family had been her only support system for a lot of years.

Randi shook her head as if to force the negative thoughts from her mind. She would focus on the house and try to remember exactly how it looked. She knew without a doubt it would be smaller than the mansion in her memory, but with six large bedrooms, wide halls and deep-set porches, it would have to be an imposing structure, even in its dilapidated state. She smiled as she remembered that wonderful porch, the clickety clack of her skates as they crossed the wooden planks, and the chorus of frogs and cicadas that wafted up to the house from the low places in the yard. That porch had been one of her favorite places in the whole world, and she'd thought of it often over the years. She felt a cold knot form in the pit of her stomach as she realized her fanciful memories were about to be replaced by the ugly reality of time and neglect.

The gates of Willow Bend now lay before her, and she was swept by a whirlwind of emotions. The sense of happiness and purpose she'd experienced these past few weeks gave way to apprehension. Doubt crept into her thoughts as she got out to unlock the gates. She inserted the key into the padlock with trembling hands. She had come here for something. Peace? Closure? Adventure? What if there was no peace? And how could she ever have closure when she still didn't know if her father was dead or alive? Was adventure really the answer at this stage of life?

She steadied her hands and turned the key. The lock opened easily, and the chain slithered through the iron fretwork. As soon as the gates were unbound, they began to swing open, beckoning her inward. Just as her skin began to crawl from the groaning and creaking that accompanied their progress, the heavy gates stilled their motion, gravity having done all it could to facilitate her entry. The gates hung partially open in the still evening air, and the only disruption to the silence around her was the drone of hungry mosquitoes darting around her face and lighting on her arms. She forced the gates wider, propping each with a piece of concrete block that had been strewn to the side, apparently for that very purpose, slapping at her vicious attackers as she went. Grateful for the refuge provided by the air-conditioning, Randi pulled the truck and camper through the gates and fixed her gaze on the rutted track that lay ahead.

———————

Hitch Williams was headed home when he noticed the open gates and the back end of a camper disappearing down the lane of

Willow Bend. It looked as if the new owners had arrived at last. Most days he drove by the entrance without a second thought, but seeing the gates open brought on a rush of memories. He'd known some good days there to be sure, but it was also where he'd watched his dad turn into a miserable drunk. Henry Moore had been the master of Willow Bend back then, as well as his father's employer. Hitch sure hoped the new owners would enjoy happier days than poor Henry Moore.

CHAPTER TWO

Randi awoke with a start and groped for the travel alarm clock beside the bed. The clock hadn't gone off yet, and it was only five am. She rolled over in disgust, realizing that it would be another hour at least before sunrise. She'd been at Willow Bend two weeks now but hadn't had a full night's sleep since her arrival. She'd been rising each morning with the sun, anxious to make use of every bit of daylight. While she'd fallen into an exhausted heap each evening, she hadn't yet been able to pull off a full night's sleep. She told herself it was because she was adjusting to new surroundings, but she didn't really believe it. She'd had a feeling of unease, practically since her arrival, but couldn't put her finger on the cause of the anxiety. She wasn't a nervous person by nature, and she wasn't used to this new and unwanted sensation. She'd served in the Air Force for heaven's sake, and she and Bill had traveled all over the world. She was experienced and competent, so it was a mystery where all of this was coming from. While it had been years since her last adventure owing to Bill's last round of illness, she refused to think it had anything to do with her age. Her mother wasn't even old yet!

The filth she'd encountered in the house had been unbelievable. Dogs had apparently slept with their owners and enjoyed the full run of the house. She'd swept up three full buckets of dust and dog hair from the first floor alone and thrown out a plethora of cots and mattresses left behind by the former occupants. Most of the furnishings were trashed beyond repair, and she planned to have a big bonfire sometime soon. It had been a rough couple of weeks, but she hoped the worst of the cleanup was behind her. She was very grateful to have the camper, as it would be many months before the house was fit for occupancy.

She stretched and rolled over, thinking about her plans for the day. She'd spent the first night at Willow Bend making lists and arranging tasks on a calendar, but she knew from previous experience that renovation wasn't an exact science. She and Bill had undertaken quite a few projects over the years, so she couldn't plead ignorance relative to the challenges associated with remodeling. Then again, Willow Bend could hardly be called a remodeling job. In fact, she feared this was going to be more of a tear- down-to-the-studs project. Randi was relieved to see that the exterior of the house had fared pretty well, considering the years of neglect, but she was beginning to realize the enormity of what would be required for the interior. Thinking about the wiring was scary, and she had no idea what she'd find if she actually ventured under the house. She would have to rely on a contractor for an expert assessment, and there was no use speculating now. The electric company had promised to come out for an evaluation on restoring power to the structure, but that had been over a week ago. By now she would believe it when she saw the power company truck in the yard, and maybe not even then.

Thank goodness for the camper and generator. Her needs were simple, but she did require a few amenities. Food wasn't a big deal. She'd used the microwave a time or two to heat up some canned beans, but mainly she'd been subsisting on peanut butter and jelly sandwiches. Over the weekend she'd splurged and baked a chicken pot pie in the oven, and the next night she'd kept the lights on for over an hour after dark. But the biggest drain on the generator was the power required for her daily shower. It was never a long affair since the camper's hot water heater left a lot to be desired, but Randi would have showered in cold water if necessary. The thought of crawling into bed unwashed was as foreign to her as speaking Chinese. Bill used to say she was the cleanest woman in six states, and he'd often teased her for the compulsion, especially while traveling abroad. How he would laugh to see how she'd been living the past two weeks! Randi felt fortunate to have water at least. While the existing power hook up hadn't been sufficient for all the camper's electrical service needs, it had been enough to power the water pump. Randi had always been adaptable and something of a minimalist, and she was glad for that now.

Just how long the house had been without electricity was a mystery. While the pole and pump near the camper appeared to be of recent vintage, the pole closest to the house was broken in half, the top portion in splinters on the ground near the back porch. The line had pulled away from the corner of the roof and lay limply in the grass. She didn't really want to know what led to the mishap with the pole. Absentee property owners could expect all manner of revelry and devilment from renters or trespassers. There was no telling what activities had taken place at Willow Bend over the years, but Randi was certain some of it had nothing to do with hunting. She was pretty sure there was a small fortune in the backyard, judging from the mounds of aluminum beer cans and glass bottles near the fire pit. Target practice was in evidence as well, and if spent shells and casings were money, she'd eat steak for a year.

In addition to the cleaning jag, or perhaps as a result of it, she'd been remembering things. Little snatches mostly, more solidly here and there. She vividly remembered the greenhouse and the potting shed for some reason. The former had been filled to the brim with Boston ferns during the winter months. She remembered her mother saying they should never be too quick to put the ferns out after Easter, lest a late frost threaten their tender fronds. She'd winced at the memory. Her mother had been "Mama" back then. She'd been more like Mommie Dearest in the years since.

The wide wraparound porch had been encircled in ferns in those days, each suspended, perfectly centered between the columns that supported the roof. Strangely, she remembered her father had gone missing while the ferns were out, and they'd moved after the ferns had been put away. Now the greenhouse had only a few unbroken panes, and the pristine white paint that covered the clapboard buildings was all gone.

Randi rolled over again and wondered for the millionth time what really happened to her dad. She couldn't conceive of anything that would have lured him away from Willow Bend and his family. Her eyelids began to droop, and she realized she was in danger of drifting off to sleep as the first rays of sun began to peek through the curtain near her bed. She had a choice to make. Nobody would know or care if she got in a couple more hours of sleep. The bed was comfortable, and the thought of languishing there indefinitely held an allure of hedonism that ran counter to her sensibilities. She lay there, precious minutes more, enjoying the feel of the well-worn sheets against her skin. As the sun rose, she roused herself to wakefulness. Randi promised herself that once Willow Bend was in order, she'd treat herself to a languid morning of rest and relaxation. That would be her reward for her considerable efforts, and it was something to look forward to. She ate a quick breakfast, slipped into her clothes and headed out to greet the day.

———————

Hitch Williams was up with the sun, preparing breakfast and packing a lunch he knew he probably wouldn't even have time to eat. He had a full day ahead of him and lots to do before a business trip scheduled for later in the week. He had three job sites to visit in three different counties, and a bid to fax over to a young, arrogant project manager for the City of Columbia. And if he managed to get all that done by a decent time, he could swing by Willow Bend to meet the new owners on the way home. He whistled for Bo and stepped outside to another muggy South Carolina summer morning.

CHAPTER THREE

Randi was screwing a light bulb into the fixture that hung in the kitchen when she heard a dog barking. Unless a stray was passing through, she guessed she had another visitor with a canine companion. She was learning that the local population didn't let a little thing like work separate them from their best friends. The wiring inspector had arrived early that morning accompanied by a yellow Lab. The electric company had rolled in after lunch with a blue tick hound riding in the cab between the two workers. Randi had not asked if this was routine, or if the dog was there in any official capacity. It had taken a few hours and another truck and crew to complete the installation of a new pole, but at last, power had been restored to the house. She'd picked up a cell phone message indicating the recommended contractor would do his best to stop by today, but she'd given up on him after six o'clock. It was nearly eight now, and Randi couldn't imagine he'd be coming by at this late hour. She hurried out to the porch on high alert, lest her visitor be of the unwanted variety.

In the dimming light she could make out a graphic on the side of the pickup that read "Williams Construction". There didn't seem to be anyone about, but a large black Lab ambled over and sniffed her curiously. He seemed friendly enough, so Randi reached out to offer him a scratch behind the ears. The dog rubbed his body against her legs to show his appreciation, pressing his large head against her to encourage her attentions. A strong voice broke the stillness of the evening air.

"Bo, get back in the truck! You'll get the lady all dirty!" Randi turned in the direction of the voice and locked gazes with one of the nicest looking men she'd seen in a while. The dog ambled away reluctantly as Randi reached up to smooth her hair with one hand and adjust her shirttail with the other.

"Hitch Williams, ma'am," the voice said, extending his hand. "I see you've made Bo's acquaintance. Sorry about that." Randi still hadn't found her voice, so the stranger spoke again. "I hope you don't mind that I was walking around the yard a few minutes," he continued.

Finally, Randi realized it was her turn to speak. "Not at all, Mr. Williams." she practically stammered. "I'm Randi Jackson, and you'll have to forgive me. My social skills have apparently rusted during my stay in the woods."

Her visitor ascended the last step and she shook his extended hand, silently berating herself for her awkwardness.

"No problem, ma'am. I hope I didn't startle you too much, showing up this late I mean." Was he slow to release her hand or was it her that lingered too long? Randi couldn't be sure, but she felt the long-forgotten heat of a blush coming on. She pulled her hand away, took a deep breath and found her voice.

"Well, I must say I wasn't expecting you this late, Mr. Williams..." her voice trailed off, though warmth and stability had returned to her tone at least. He was a good foot taller than her, and quite imposing.

"Please call me Hitch, Ms. Jackson." he said with a smile. "Believe me, I am well aware that contractors don't have the best reputation to start with, so I try to do what I say I'm gonna do. I left word that I would do my best to come by today, and according to my watch, I made it with 4 hours to spare." He pointed to his watch face for emphasis, and Randi couldn't help but smile. Grateful for the dimming light considering the mess she must be, she hoped her wit would make up for any deficiencies.

"Ok, Mr. Williams, I mean, Hitch. It's duly noted that you arrived on the date expected, but the jury's still out on anything after that!" She thought she saw a glimpse of appreciation in his eyes, so perhaps she wasn't quite as fumbling as she felt.

"Fair enough, Ms. Jackson, I'll do my best to impress you." Hitch declared, offering a mocking bow.

"Call me Randi." she replied, motioning him inside to escape the mosquitoes. It would be dark in a few minutes, and they had yet to discuss his business here. She looked around self-consciously as he stepped out of the entry hall into the front room. Randi's thoughts surprised her. How she would have loved to entertain this man in better surroundings! She chastised herself again for the direction of her thoughts as she checked his hand for a wedding ring. Good heavens, she thought. He's a perfect stranger!

"You'll have to excuse the place." Randi said, dragging a chair out from under a battered table, motioning for him to have a seat. "As you can see, things need some work around here."

Hitch pulled out a chair for her rather than sitting immediately, offering it as gallantly as if it were the last seat on a crowded bus. He handed her a business card as they sat.

"You don't have to excuse the place on my account. Projects like this keep me in business, you know. Williams Construction Company at your service, ma'am, specializing in historical restoration and reproduction."

He opened a small notebook he'd pulled from his shirt pocket and scribbled down a few notes, ceiling height and the like, she guessed. The man appeared to be sixty-ish, and she found herself studying him unabashedly as he wrote. Her inspection was focused on the fit of his jeans when she realized to her horror that he was no longer writing in the notebook. He was watching her intently, and he seemed amused. It took everything Randi had not to look away in embarrassment as she wondered how long since he'd put away the notebook. Her response was weak to say the least, but it was all she could manage considering her discomfort.

"I'd offer you a cold drink, Mr. Williams, but I don't think my refrigerator is running."

CHAPTER FOUR

itch ended up staying at the house for nearly an hour to get the information he'd need to make recommendations and offer cost estimates. He'd been friendly, but professional, and took a couple of opportunities to share his suggestions for the project. As for Randi, she was just grateful he'd had the good grace not to comment on her brazen inspection of his attributes, and she even dared to hope he'd written off the social lapse to her obvious lack of sleep and comforts. He'd promised to return the following week to present his proposal for the restoration, and she was looking forward to the appointment. She even made sure to pin him down regarding a specific date and time so she could be prepared with a suitable presentation of her own.

Then, as if their next meeting hadn't been enough to contemplate, he'd made a startling revelation as he stepped off the porch. He told her his dad had been employed at Willow Bend in the early sixties, and that he himself had enjoyed many happy days exploring the farm and helping his dad with the chores. He went on to say that he remembered how beautiful Willow Bend had once been, and he was really looking forward to bringing her back to her former status. Randi had been shocked by this news, and she knew she'd stared at him a few moments before replying. She couldn't be sure, but she thought she even heard him mutter something about seeing a ghost as she pulled herself together and thanked him for his time. As she waved goodbye and watched the taillights of the pickup disappear into the trees, she cursed herself for her silence. Why hadn't she just told him who she was? Willow Bend had been her home a lifetime ago, and yet she had told no one, not even the attorney that handled the closing. It was almost as if it was somebody else's life.

She turned out the few lights in the house and picked her way to the camper with a sorry flashlight that needed new batteries. The canned tuna she'd planned to have for supper held no interest for her, so she took a quick shower and climbed into bed. She hoped sleep would come quickly tonight. Instead, she laid there for hours thinking about the fact that Hitch Williams could very well provide a link to her past. She remembered a tall, lanky boy she'd seen back in those days, though she'd never actually talked to him. Her mother had been very strict with her, and she'd never been allowed to interact with any of the people who worked at Willow Bend. She remembered watching from the window of her room as the workers gathered on pay day. Each week they'd formed a line, black and white, waiting patiently for her father to press a small roll of bills into each hand. Sometimes, she'd helped her father count out the bills the night before. She would roll them up and he'd secure the rolls with thin rubber bands. Her mother had complained that the money was dirty, and Randi shouldn't be handling it. Her father would wink at her and smile, whispering that it might be dirty, but mama sure liked his dirty old money. She'd never told her mother he'd said that. It was a secret just between the two of them.

She was roused from her memories by a single tear that had formed in the corner of her eye. She allowed it to spill over the rim and run down her cheek unchecked. It had been a long time since she'd cried. She closed her eyes tightly, blocking the outlet for any more, willing herself back to the here and now, and the reality of the moment. A crescent moon peeked around the edge of the curtain, doing its best to illuminate the interior of the camper. She stared at it intently, just as she'd done dozens of times over the last fifty years, wondering if her father was somewhere, looking at the same moon and thinking of her. She'd been lucky enough to see the moon from so many places, sometimes with Bill and sometimes alone. She'd seen it on safari on the savannas of Africa. She'd seen it from a beach in Mexico and a mountaintop in Colorado. She'd seen the same moon hanging over Europe and Asia, yet the tiny, silvery crescent that hung over Willow Bend seemed more intense and glorious than all the other moonrises she'd ever witnessed anywhere else. Randi stared and stared, fixed on the unwavering light of that sliver, willing exhaustion to claim her consciousness.

Finding no sleep or relief from her thoughts, Randi sat up to search for a dry read. She knew she had a bad novel around here somewhere. Perhaps that would do the trick. She had a big day ahead of her tomorrow, as Hitch had given instructions to inventory any other structures on the property that might be scavenged for materials. He claimed that abandoned buildings were still his best source for reclaimed wood, mantels and interesting doors, so she'd promised to take a look. She wasn't aware of anything beyond the outbuildings within sight of the yard, but Hitch had encouraged her to explore. Now that she knew of his childhood, she realized he could know something she didn't. She finally felt herself drifting off as she was going over her grocery list in her head. Maybe she would even go to that little restaurant she'd seen in town....

———————

A few miles down the road from Willow Bend, Hitch rolled over and punched the pillow again. Sleep had eluded him so far, in spite of another exhausting day. He'd rushed from appointment to appointment, returned phone calls, ordered materials and checked on three job sites. It had been a normal day right up until the time he'd met Randi Jackson. What in the world was her story? Why would a woman like that come to the edge of the earth to take on a project like Willow Bend? The place had been abandoned for years, and the house was in such a sorry state that he wondered if he'd even be able to bring it back from the brink. He wondered for the tenth time that night what kind of woman would willingly move to the sticks with only the spare amenities offered by a camper. It was a puzzle alright. There didn't seem to be a man in the picture. From everything he could tell, she was the sole owner of Willow Bend, lock, stock and rotting barrel. Could it be that he'd finally stumbled across an interesting woman? He thought about the relationships he'd had since he lost his wife. There hadn't been many, nor had there been anything particularly memorable about any of them. There was the teacher from the elementary school a few years back. She'd made it clear she was looking for a husband, so he'd broken it off quickly once she made her intentions known. There was a widow from the next town he'd seen off and on over the years, but she'd grown tired of the status quo and had recently remarried. There had been a few one night stands along the way, but they hadn't exactly been appropriate company for his daughter and young grandson. In short, things had been pretty slow in the fifteen years since Barbara's death, and he'd just about given up on being seriously interested in anyone ever again. Randi Jackson. He said her name aloud in the darkness and repeated it for good measure. Could she reignite something he'd thought long dead? Could be. He made a mental note to ask Hal Crews about her the next time he saw him. As the town's only lawyer, there wasn't much Hal wouldn't know about property sales and estate business. Yes, he'd do some inquiring about this mystery lady. Hitch resolved that Randi Jackson wouldn't be a mystery for long.

CHAPTER FIVE

R andi was about to call it a day and head back to the camper when she came upon the little house. She would never have seen it at all had it not been for the fact that the sun was low in the sky and cast a glare upon a windowpane exposed by a broken shutter. The house was slightly set back in some dense woods bordering a small field near the edge of the property. Vines, bushes, and thick branches concealed all but the very front of the structure, and it looked as if the forest was about to swallow it in an attempt to wipe out any signs of civilized life. Randi consulted the plat she'd been given at the closing. She could find no mark to indicate the presence of an additional house on the property, yet it was clearly within the boundary. The aerial map she'd requested from the county office indicated a sloping descent to a narrow branch of water, the path of which was designated as the property line. The house couldn't have been more than fifty feet from the property line, but clearly it was on her side. Hitch had been right to suggest there were other buildings on the property, and Randi's heart pounded in her chest as she considered the implications of the discovery. Flashlight in hand, she resolved to explore this unexpected find.

Thankful for the fresh batteries she remembered to install just that morning, she picked her way through the underbrush, forcing the bushes and briars away from the front steps with her boot. As she mounted the porch, she noticed the front door had been secured with a heavy lock that hung between two hasps, nailed to the door face on one side and the door frame on the other. She looked around to see if there was a key hanging nearby. Finding none, she gingerly ran her fingers across the top of the door frame, hoping to get lucky. Damn! How could she get in?

The afternoon light was getting dimmer by the minute, and she switched on the flashlight to allow a closer inspection of the lock. Her heart raced anew as she realized that while the door appeared to be solid, the door frame had some termite damage that might prove useful. Randi raced to the truck for a screwdriver, already plotting a follow up with a tire tool if her initial attempt wasn't successful. As it turned out, the screwdriver was hardly necessary. She barely got the tip positioned behind the top edge of the hasp when a foot-long section broke out of the door frame. The section held fast to the hasp, and she folded it back toward the door. Now that the lock was useless, she turned the rusty knob and pulled with all her might. The heavy door dragged across the wide planks of the porch, but at last her efforts yielded an opening large enough for access. Heart pounding, she entered, grasping the flashlight hard enough to leave an imprint on her palm.

It was dreadfully dark inside, except for the little patch of light that came in through the panes exposed by the broken shutter. She walked back outside and slipped the tip of the screwdriver between the simple plank shutters accessible from the porch. They too, gave away easily, and precious pools of light flooded the musty interior. She urged herself forward, despite her trepidation, resolute in her intention to complete the exploration before dark. The sun was beginning its descent, and she'd heard a rumble or two in the distance. The pattern of evening storms had continued unabated since her arrival at Willow Bend, and all signs pointed to more of the same.

Except for the cobwebs and dust one might expect, the interior was remarkably tidy. After going through barns and sheds filled with rubbish and discarded items for most of the day, she was surprised to find this building hadn't been used for storage. In fact, as she swept the flashlight's beam around the room, she realized there was no evidence to suggest the former occupants had left with intent of relocation. The furnishings were in place, and there were a couple of pictures hanging on the walls. There were even curtains at the windows, their dusty folds drawn aside by frayed, but sturdy, cords.

As far as she could tell, the house consisted of three rooms, with the front door opening into the largest. There was a brick fireplace at one end of the room. A door along the rear wall of the room was made of heavy planks and bolted shut. Randi presumed it to be an exterior door leading to another porch or to a kitchen, as many old dwellings had a separate cook shed to protect the house in case of fire. The spare furnishings of the front room consisted of a worn couch, an upright piano, a rocking chair, and an ancient Singer sewing machine and cabinet. There was a neat stack of newspapers sitting on the hearth, but there were no logs or ashes to indicate the fireplace had been used. A cloud of dust rose up as she leafed through the folded newspapers. There were a dozen or so, all editions of The State newspaper, dating from May, June and July of 1965. She made a mental note of the date and wondered if there was any significance. Her father had disappeared in the summer that same year.

The two smaller rooms were to the left of the front door and were accessed by a single doorway opposite the fireplace. The larger of the two contained a bed, dressing table and washstand. The smaller room was accessed through the larger one and held what was obviously a child's bed, and a tiny table and chair, complete with a miniature china tea set. Randi's heart skipped a beat as she focused on the pattern revealed as she wiped away a thick coating of dust with her thumb. If memory served, she'd had a set just like it. The dishes had been a gift from her father on her 5th birthday, and he'd pretended to drink from the tiny cups on more than one occasion. She shook off the memory and was about to leave the room when the beam caught a glint of hardware on the wall. Closer inspection revealed that it was a tiny doorknob, not unlike the pull you would find on the doors of kitchen cabinets. She pulled it open and discovered that the room was smaller because it had been walled off to create a closet. Four plain uniform dresses hung on a wooden rod, their starched, white crispness blotched and stained by time and insects. There were no other clothes in the closet, but the beam revealed a small willow basket on the floor beneath the dresses. Randi bent and pulled it out to better examine it. As soon as she touched it, a memory burst into her consciousness.

She was sitting on the floor at her house, watching a dark-skinned woman as she ran an iron back and forth across one of Daddy's shirts. She could tell it was his shirt because the cuff of the long arm nearly met the floor. There was a basket on the floor behind the woman, and every now and then she rocked it with her foot. There was noise coming from the basket. The woman had her back to her, so she crept over to see what was in it. Randi was on her hands and knees about to reach out and touch the baby that was smiling at her from the basket, when her mother shouted, picked her up and hurried from the room. As her mother carried her away, Randi looked back at the woman holding the iron. There was something terrible about the woman's face, and Randi shrieked with fright.

Randi returned the basket to the closet with a shaking hand, and quickly shut the door. Why had the basket elicited such a disturbing memory? Who had lived here? Why didn't she ever remember seeing this house? She'd been out riding with her father all over Willow Bend, yet Randi had no memory of this place. The rumbling of thunder had grown louder, and Randi could hear the wind slapping tree branches against the roof. She made her way to the front room quickly, sweeping the flashlight's beam across the walls as she went. It was then she saw something on the mantle. Inpatient with her own curiosity in the face of an approaching storm, she stalked over to investigate the object that had caught her eye. Her heart stopped when she brushed the dust from the face of a framed photograph of her father sitting on the steps of Willow Bend. As soon as her heart started beating again, she snatched up a small book that lay near the photo on the mantle and dashed out the door. Heavy plops of rain chased her all the way to the truck.

CHAPTER SIX

B y nine o'clock the next morning, Randi was sitting in an airport waiting for a connecting flight to Ft. Lauderdale. There was only one person who could address the questions raised by yesterday's discoveries, and she intended to have answers today. Randi had not told her mother the nature of her sudden visit; only that she would be passing through the area and wanted to stop by. She'd learned through bitter experience that it was never a good idea to tip your hand to Lavinia, particularly if you were on a fishing expedition. Given enough warning, her mother could serve up a canned speech with a side of spin that would make a politician proud. The trick was to catch her flat-footed and unprepared.

It had been difficult to speak with Lavinia by telephone with burning questions on her mind, but Randi had somehow managed to pull off a nonchalant and friendly tone as she requested that her mother make herself available for a visit. Lavinia had indicated she'd be missing bridge club in deference to Randi's request, but assured her daughter that she considered it a worthy sacrifice. Randi thanked her for her graciousness and assured her that her time and consideration were appreciated. An outsider listening to the conversation would never have guessed they were overhearing dialog between a mother and daughter. So polite, so sanitized, so sterile was the exchange that one could easily imagine having the same conversation with the social secretary for some foreign head of state.

Randi smiled in self-congratulation as she realized she'd made a good decision by withholding the news of her acquisition of Willow Bend. Her mother had absolutely no idea what Randi had been up to these past several months, and she'd be floored when she learned of her daughter's return to her childhood home. As far as Lavinia knew, Willow Bend was nothing more to her daughter than a distant memory, and Randi couldn't help but relish yet another opportunity to pull her mother's chain. She knew it was childish, but she had a feeling what she'd done this time would eclipse any of her previous campaigns to cause her mother vexation. Joining the Air Force after college had been one thing. Marrying a college history professor with no particular claim-to-fame had been another. Buying Willow Bend and restoring it would be a new high for Randi relative to needling her mother, and she was anxious to get on with the reveal party. Randi had seen her mother transform from charming to bitch in less than thirty seconds on many occasions, and she doubted she would be treated to anything less today.

Lavinia Whiddon Moore was in her early thirties when Randi's father had vanished from their lives. She'd been what was called a stewardess back in the early days of passenger flight, and Randi supposed it had been a fascinating way to meet people and see the world back in the fifties. Lavinia had met and married Henry Moore in 1957 after a whirlwind courtship, and Randi had been born the following year. In the years since Lavinia had taken her daughter to California in 1965, Randi's childhood had been a sidecar to her mother's endless parade of boyfriends, fiancés and husbands. Lavinia had divorced two husbands and buried two more in the last thirty years, and Randi wasn't at all sure about her present status. The last update was an engagement to a golf pro from a senior community in Miami. Lavinia had provided this information at the time of their last telephone conversation some months back, but she'd assured Randi she was keeping her condo in Ft. Lauderdale just in case things didn't work out. And if Randi knew her mother, there was a Plan B man stashed away somewhere too, just in case.

The intercom sounded the alert for passenger boarding, and Randi gathered up her purse and the small overnight bag she'd packed, just in case. Perhaps she was more like her mother than she realized, preferring to err on the side of caution when it came to contingency planning. Randi had not gone as far as making a hotel reservation though, for she fully intended to keep her visit short and sweet, catching the last flight north, if at all possible. Her mother would likely offer the spare room, assuming the meeting didn't turn hostile, but Randi was pretty sure a few hours of her mother's company would be all she could stand.

As she headed to the gate, Randi felt some apprehension about her purpose and the day that lay ahead. Would her mother be able to shed any light on the little house and the curious items she'd found inside? Had she discovered something of interest in her quest to uncover the facts surrounding her father's disappearance? Would she be sorry she asked? This last question would fuel her thoughts for the duration of the flight.

CHAPTER SEVEN

I t was early afternoon before Randi made her destination. They'd circled the airport nearly an hour before landing, due to some security issue in the terminal. She stumbled out to the cabstand with a few dozen other aggravated passengers, thankful at least she didn't have the added burden of a trip to baggage claim. The taxi ride to her mother's condo was even more miserable. The driver finally confessed that the cab's air conditioning wasn't working just about the time they pulled onto the interstate, and Randi couldn't help but remark that the information would have been more useful before her cab selection. It wasn't as if she had an alternative at this point, so she rolled down the window and resolved to make the best of it. By the time Randi arrived at the condo, her hair looked as if it had been styled with an eggbeater. She rifled through her purse for taxi fare and fished out a lipstick she hoped would provide a little touch up. She jammed the cash at the driver, stepped out into the street, and fluffed her hair with her fingers as best she could.

Apparently, she'd just missed a south Florida rainstorm, and the steamy heat from the pavement finished off any lingering freshness from her morning shower. Randi sighed in disgust as she felt the telltale droplets of perspiration beading on her skin and sliding to points south. She swore under her breath. She didn't have any problem with sweating due to hard work or exercise, but she most definitely had a problem with sweating for no good reason. As she walked up the sidewalk to her mother's door, she couldn't help but feel disadvantaged. A position of weakness was exactly what you didn't want when facing off with Lavinia, and Randi willed herself to shake off her discouraging thoughts.

The door swung open before Randi could even ring the doorbell. "Miranda, darling, how good to see you!", Lavinia gushed. "Look at you, all travel worn! You must be exhausted!"

Randi offered her own greeting as her mother looked her over, raising an eyebrow reproachfully. Randi was more than a little familiar with the tactic. It was meant to make her feel like an urchin, grubby and un-coiffed, and therefore, not as good. She had been the recipient of her mother's thinly veiled disappointment many times, and Randi had to smile at the absolute predictability of her mother's reception. There were constants in this life; the moon, the tides, Lavinia's superiority.

Randi was ushered into the cool interior of the foyer, Lavinia's heels tapping on the wide tiles as she led the way. Her mother was immaculate, as always, dressed in a sea foam silk pantsuit and matching high heeled sandals. Manicured and pedicured in a pale shell pink, Lavinia was the picture of a pampered lady of leisure.

"Mother, you look absolutely wonderful. I hope you're feeling as good as you look.", Randi complimented, as her mother led her into the living room and gestured to the couch. Lavinia patted the cushion beside her and reached over for what seemed to be a compulsory hug as she answered.

"Well, I do fine as long as I don't stop to think about how old I am.", her mother laughed. "Naturally I have a few aches and pains now and then, but I've been very fortunate. My doctor says I have the constitution of a much younger woman, so I expect to be around a good while longer if he's any judge of the matter." Lavinia leaned back into the plush cushions of the couch for the moment, striking a relaxed pose to mask the state of alert betrayed by her sharp eyes.

"Would you care for a cold drink, dear? Forgive my manners, as I should have asked you straight away!" Randi was thirsty, but she didn't think her hands would be steady enough to hold a glass. She felt like a coiled spring, and it was all she could do not to unload on her mother in a heated rush. She opted for a lie instead.

"No thanks, I grabbed a cold drink before I left the airport." A few more minutes passed, Lavinia inquiring about Randi's health and emotional state since the loss of her husband, and Randi, responding that all was well and inquiring about her mother's engagement. Lavinia confided that she was having second thoughts about the golf pro from Miami and was reconsidering the decision to relinquish the carefree life she'd enjoyed in recent years. Randi, of course, encouraged her mother to follow her instincts if she had the slightest bit of doubt.

By the time that conversation had run its course, Randi was feeling a little less jangled and more in control of her thoughts. It was time to broach the subject matter at hand. She knew her next words would bring the pleasantries to a screeching halt, and she steeled herself for the bitter words that would likely follow her inquiries. Her mother didn't like to talk about the past and she'd never been cooperative when it came to Randi's questions. Over time, Randi had learned to avoid the subject entirely, and in fact this would be her first foray into forbidden territory in over thirty years. She reached into her purse and drew out the two items that had given rise to her visit, and her voice quavered only slightly as she met her mother's questioning gaze.

"Mother, I want you to tell me everything you know about my father's disappearance." Randi saw her mother's jaw tighten as she drew up her chin defiantly. Lavinia was marshaling her defenses and calling up the old sound bites when Randi hit her with the question that would make the old playbook obsolete.

"And by the way, Mother, who is Lisette?"

CHAPTER EIGHT

The seconds ticked by as Randi watched her mother's face transform from ashen shock to stony stiffness. As the color returned to Lavinia's features, Randi dared to hope she'd finally stumbled across a puzzle piece that would force her mother to deal with her as an adult. After all, Randi had some evidence there were problems in the marriage.

"Miranda, for God's sake, why are you dredging all of that up again? What do you expect to accomplish with your questions?" Lavinia sighed and threw up her hands.

"You didn't answer the question, Mother. Who is Lisette?", Randi demanded calmly.

Her mother pursed her lips like a petulant child and crossed her arms in a defensive pose.

"I'm not going to be drawn into a pointless conversation about things best left forgotten.", Lavinia declared.

"Best forgotten by who, Mother? Who is Lisette?", Randi repeated, each word spoken with deliberation, lest Lavinia think she could weaken her daughter's resolve. Randi pushed the framed photo toward her mother. "This is a picture of Daddy. Do you know it?"

Lavinia looked at the object, feigning a nonchalance Randi was certain she didn't feel. Randi watched her mother carefully but could read little from her expression.

"Yes, it's Henry, so what? I've never seen the photo before.", she replied, leaning back into the cushions in resignation to Randi's questions. Now her mother looked bored rather than angry.

"Don't you want to know where I got this photo?", Randi queried. Her mother's attitude confused her.

Lavinia shrugged her shoulders. "I assume you got it from your grandparents years ago."

Randi opened the small volume of verses and pointed to an inscription inside the front cover. "What if I told you I got the photo from a mantle of a small house at Willow Bend. This book was lying beside it."

Lavinia jolted forward, blanching for a moment as she stared at the book in Randi's outstretched hand. At last her mother took it from her with a trembling hand.

"Why are you doing this to me, Miranda? Are you deliberately being cruel?", she whined.

Randi watched as her mother read the words her husband had apparently written to another woman. 'To Lisette, with much love, Henry'

Lavinia closed the book and dropped it to the coffee table.

"You must really hate me to bring a thing like that into my house.", her mother shouted accusingly.

Randi didn't look away but softened her tone a bit.

"No, Mama, I only want to understand." The two women sat there for a few minutes in silence, Lavinia staring at her daughter through the cold mask that had replaced her shock, and Randi wearing what she hoped was an expression of determination and strength. Finally, the silence was broken by Lavinia's inevitable question.

"Miranda, what on earth were you doing at Willow Bend?"

Randi took her mother's hands in hers and made firm eye contact.

"I own Willow Bend now, Mama." It took only a few seconds for the declaration to sink in.

"That's not possible, Miranda. You couldn't afford to buy a place like that on a teacher's salary! What do you take me for?", she demanded, pulling her hands away. Lavinia's demeanor had changed quite drastically, and she was quite agitated now. Randi knew it was important to keep her responses controlled and her mind sharp. This was causing Lavinia a great deal of discomfort, but Randi intended to follow through despite the protests that were sure to come.

"I was lucky enough to buy 300 acres and the house. I'm having Willow Bend restored.", Randi said quietly.

Lavinia stared at her vacantly for a moment, processing this unexpected information. She seemed to be far away, lost in her own memories of a previous life.

"I'll start with the house, of course", Randi continued, "then I'll restore the barn and other outbuildings as I can."

Lavinia seemed to lurch back to the present, and for a moment Randi thought she caught a glimpse of fear in her mother's eyes.

"You can't mean all of that's still standing after all these years!" she exclaimed. Lavinia jumped to her feet and stalked to the kitchen, her movement a metaphor for the widening chasm between mother and daughter.

Randi followed her step-for-step, eager to press forward while her mother was on the defensive. Lavinia filled a teakettle with water and busied herself with selecting cups and saucers from the cupboard. She kept her face averted as she rummaged for tea bags and sugar.

"Mother, I have obviously struck a nerve here, but I want you to understand that I'm only asking for information. This isn't meant to hurt you!" Lavinia didn't respond, so Randi pressed on as her mother opened the refrigerator for a carton of cream.

"For God's sake, Mother, would you please give me the courtesy of a straight answer for once in your life?"

Lavinia slammed the door so hard the jelly jars rattled on the shelf. Her mother narrowed her eyes and fairly spat her bitter retort.

"Fine, Miranda. Have it your own way. You always do. It's clear that you've come here on a mission, so I won't disappoint you. You say you only want information?"

Randi nodded mutely, fully aware that she had crossed into territory from which there could be no retreat. Randi started to speak, but her mother held up her hand in protest.

"I'll do the talking from here on, Miranda. I'll tell you what you want to know, but then I want your promise that you'll leave this alone once and for all. I must further insist that after today we will never speak of these matters again. Do you agree to my terms?"

Lavinia's eyes flashed nothing but anger, and Randi knew from experience that it would do no good to argue.

"Do you agree?", her mother hissed impatiently. "I want your promise on this, Miranda. Do I have it?"

A distant chime sounded from somewhere down the hall as Randi's heart pounded in her chest.

"I promise.", she heard herself whisper.

CHAPTER NINE

The trip back had been nothing less than tortuous. Randi and her mother had said their goodbyes within an hour of arrival, but a violent line of thunderstorms had caused delays for all departing flights. As a result, she'd missed her connecting flight, and she'd languished at the Atlanta airport on standby for hours. She was just about to head down to the car rental desks when the ticket agent called her name over the intercom. There was one seat left on the last flight to Columbia, and she'd been lucky enough to get it.

The turbulence had been terrible, and by the time they touched down she had a headache and a queasy feeling that required immediate attention. Randi dug through her overnight bag for some pink bismuth tablets and threw back the tepid remains of the bottled water she'd picked up before boarding in Ft. Lauderdale. A carbonated drink would have been better, but she doubted there were any vendors open at this late hour. It was just after midnight, but she wouldn't be hitting the sack any time soon. It was over an hour drive back to Willow Bend, and she was as tired as she'd ever been. She'd been up since five am the previous day, and she was flagging to say the least. Randi dragged herself to the airport parking lot, scanning the sea of vehicles for the familiar silhouette of her old truck.

Beyond her physical exhaustion, there was the matter of Lavinia's disclosure. Her mother had accomplished her tale without the vaguest hint of emotion, and upon the conclusion of it, had announced that she was tired, and Randi could show herself out at her convenience. Randi assured her mother that she was anxious to get back, and after the obligatory entreaty to stay in touch, she was on her way. With her mind reeling, she remembered little of the cab ride to the airport. The flight had been consumed with piecing together what she knew with Lavinia's version of events, and by now all emotion had been replaced by a dull, empty feeling that threatened to engulf her.

The simple fact was her father had deserted his wife and child in favor of a family Randi never knew he had, and that awful truth ran counter to every fanciful scenario she'd imagined over the years. According to her mother, his departure was declared a disappearance rather than a desertion to protect the family during those times of racial unrest, as his lover was a "woman of color". Lavinia had even disclosed the existence of a child from that union, and Randi wondered about the baby in the willow basket once again. Lavinia had insisted it was the child's birth that had finally forced her husband to a decision, and he'd taken his new family to Canada in the summer of 1965. She added that as far as she knew, that's where he'd lived out the rest of his life. Randi had digested this information in shocked silence, finally asking a question or two once she found her voice. In time, Randi knew she would come to terms with this altered reality, but right now, she was too tired to think about it anymore.

She found her truck after a considerable hike and climbed inside with a rush of relief. The confines of the cab wrapped Randi in security and familiarity, and she felt some of the day's tensions ebb away as she drank in the unique smells and textures. She ran her hands across the well-worn steering wheel cover, remembering the day she and Bill had attempted to refurbish the truck's aging interior. They'd been living in Arizona then, and had selected a Native American print for the seat covers. The matching steering wheel cover proved too large and Bill had finally secured it with a thin leather thong that he'd wrapped round and round. Randi had teased him that the truck was running "on a string and a prayer", yet they'd managed to have so many wonderful adventures with it. Bill had lovingly patched it up more times than Randi could count, and she hadn't had the heart to sell it after his death. The truck was one of the last vestiges of her former life, and she just wasn't ready to give it up.

Randi put the key in the ignition to crank it up, just as she'd done thousands of times before. This time, of all times, nothing happened. She tried again with an anxious fluttering in her stomach as she assessed her deteriorating situation. While there were plenty of cars in the parking lot, there weren't many people around at this hour. Cold fear shot through her as she realized she would be at the mercy of whoever the auto club might send to her aid, and she reached under the seat and brushed her fingers against the cold steel barrel of the 38 revolver that lay on the floorboard. Randi sat back up and tried the ignition again, chiding herself for her overactive imagination. No luck. She reached into her purse for her cell phone and popped open the glove box for the auto club card. She dialed the 800 number and got two rings before a warning beep indicated the phone's battery was low. Damn! The phone hadn't been holding a proper charge for weeks, and she'd been meaning to replace it. Too bad that task hadn't been higher on her priority list! Randi dug through her purse hoping the charger was there, knowing even as she rummaged that it was likely on the counter in the camper.

She was just about to cry out of sheer exhaustion and frustration when someone knocked on the driver's side window and scared her half to death. She was startled, so it took a few moments for recognition to register in her brain. Randi had only met the man once, but he'd made an impression. She rubbed her eyes and looked at him again to be sure. Hitch Williams was standing right beside her truck.

CHAPTER TEN

There had been a few times in Randi's life when she'd awakened on a Monday morning to ask herself what the hell she'd been thinking. This was one of those times.

True, she'd just enjoyed one of the best weekends of her life, but now she was riddled with feelings of guilt and uncertainty. She'd convinced herself of the irrationality of her feelings of disloyalty to Bill by Saturday morning. After all, Bill had often voiced his hope that she would be able to move on to another fulfilling relationship after he was gone, and Hitch certainly seemed like a nice man. It was last night's events that had her in a twist, and now she was scrambling for a way to gracefully extricate herself from the web of omissions she'd constructed over the course of her brief acquaintance with Hitch Williams.

Hitch and Randi had grown close, to say the least, since he'd rescued her from the airport on Friday night. He'd been on the same flight from Atlanta, having just returned from a couple of days

of consulting work with an architectural firm in Marietta. Randi
had not volunteered the nature of her travels, and mercifully, Hitch
hadn't asked. It had only taken him a few minutes to diagnose the
problem and pronounce the truck dead. He'd brushed off her protests to drop her by an airport hotel, insisting that Willow Bend was
on his way and he'd be grateful for the company. He'd collected her
belongings and deposited them in his truck before she could mount
another wave of objections, and Randi had climbed in without a
backward glance.

They'd talked non-stop, all the way home, both behaving as
if they'd just been released from a stiff term in solitary. He told
Randi all about his daughter, his five-year- old grandson, and the
wife he'd lost years earlier in a car crash. Randi told him about
all the different places she'd lived, her time in the Air Force, and
how she'd met and married Bill, only to lose him to cancer two
years ago. She unburdened her soul about her regrets over her
childlessness, her fears for the future, and the loneliness of the
present. She told him everything except who she was and why
she had returned to Willow Bend. Somehow, she wasn't ready to
give up that piece of her history. Randi told herself that would
come later, after she knew Hitch better and had a chance to process Lavinia's story.

They'd arrived at the turn off to Willow Bend during the driving rains and gusting winds of yet another thunderstorm. Hitch
never even slowed down, insisting that an unsecured camper was
no place to be in violent weather. Randi hadn't voiced a single word
of protest and within minutes they'd turned down a desolate road a
mile or so from her property. He'd explained they could stay at his

camp until the weather improved, and she'd been as nervous and excited as a schoolgirl as she contemplated the possibilities.

Randi had never been so grateful for the plan-ahead spirit that had led her to pack the unused overnight bag. Hitch's "camp" turned out to be a lovely cabin on the banks of a beautiful Carolina cypress pond, and it was easy to blame the charming setting when one night turned into two. They'd fished on Saturday morning and cavorted with Bo in the early afternoon. In the heat of the evening, they'd retreated to the cooler confines of the cabin, where Hitch prepared grits, fried catfish and wine for supper. The food, wine and good company soon conspired against them, and Hitch and Randi had surrendered to the inexorable yearnings that had been mounting since their arrival at the cabin. Even now, lying in her bed all alone, Randi was warmed and heartened by the memory of their lovemaking, and she dared to hope she could look forward to another such weekend very soon.

Pushing the memory aside, she focused her attention on the matter at hand. How would she tell Hitch that Randi Jackson, the woman he spent the weekend with, was really Miranda Moore, the little girl who lived at Willow Bend many years before? She should have told him last night while he was sharing childhood recollections. The photograph she'd used to confront her mother had fallen out of her bag as she was gathering her things to leave. Hitch had picked it up and stared at it for a moment, recognition registering on his handsome features. Randi was shocked and silent as he began to speak, and now she was vehemently sorry she hadn't taken the opportunity to correct his assumption that she'd found the photo at Willow Bend. The fact that she'd found it would be secondary to the fact that the man in the photo was her father, especially after he shared the history of its origin.

Hitch had taken the picture with a new Brownie camera he'd received for his 12th birthday. He'd been taking pictures around the farm while his dad was working, and according to Hitch, Mr. Henry had asked him to take his photo on the front steps of the house. Hitch said Mr. Moore was a kind and generous man and very well-liked by everyone in town. Naturally, Hitch felt proud to take the photo, and was pleased when he was presented with five dollars for development expenses. Randi was just about to interject with her confession when Hitch remarked that Mrs. Moore had been another matter. He related that a week later, he'd attempted to deliver the photograph, only to be dismissed and insulted by Mrs. Moore's suggestion that that he remove his poor, white trash existence from her porch. Hitch had smiled rather bitterly when he told Randi that he hadn't bothered to tell the woman that it was in fact his family that owned Willow Bend prior to the War Between the States. Randi felt a wave of nausea rise in her throat when Hitch recalled that Mr. Henry had gone missing just a few weeks after he'd given him the photograph. Randi had mumbled a hasty excuse about not feeling well, and asked Hitch to take her home. The drive back had been accomplished with little conversation, mostly consisting of her thanks for the rescue and the weekend, and his assurance that he would call a buddy in Columbia to see about the truck.

As Randi dressed for the day, she couldn't help but wonder if she was reading things all wrong. Was Hitch interested in a relationship, or was it just sex and nothing more? And if he was looking for something meaningful, could he accept the fact that she was the daughter of the woman who'd ordered him off her porch so many years ago? They'd had a great time together. Surely he'd be able to see that she was nothing like her mother. She applied a light coat of lipstick and cast a critical eye on her reflection, berating herself for the continuing post-mortem on the weekend. What the hell? If it was just about sex, so be it. At least the sex had been good, and there would be nothing compromised by disclosing her lineage. While the thought seemed to satisfy her head, she couldn't say it brought much comfort to her heart.

———————

Hitch got in his truck and headed out to check on a job in the next county. It had been quite a weekend, but now it was back to the grind. He had a full plate this week and would be stretched thin, even without the prospect of a re-invigorated social life. Randi Jackson was attractive, fun and available. Even though she'd seemed a little subdued by the end of the weekend, Hitch couldn't help but feel positive about the budding relationship. Still, he wondered about the sudden change of demeanor he'd seen last night. Things were moving fast, and she may have been worried about the impression made by spending the weekend with a man she hardly knew. For that matter, she could be wondering about him spending the weekend with a woman he barely knew. He reasoned one or the other was the most plausible theory and resolved to reassure her the moment he got a chance.

Hitch hadn't been this excited about a woman in a long time, and he was going to do all he could to keep things on track. The first order of business was a visit with his old football buddy. Small town lawyers were a font a knowledge, especially after a couple of beers. Hitch would find out what there was to know about Randi Jackson just as soon as he could arrange a long overdue lunch with an old friend. He picked up his cell and scrolled through the list of recent calls. With any luck he could check on his job and be back to the cafe in time for the lunch crowd. Hal never missed a day unless he was in court, so there was a good chance Hitch could find out what he knows sooner rather than later. Hitch smiled when Hal answered on the second ring.

CHAPTER ELEVEN

Randi ate her breakfast with little interest as she read the newspaper she'd picked up on her travels. She couldn't say if it was simply the inevitable low that naturally follows a high, or if this really was that boring of a day. In either case she felt a melancholy mood organizing and she was searching for preemptive diversion. The camper seemed smaller than usual and she very much needed to get out and do something. Randi knew no good would come of lying around and feeling sorry for herself, and it would be great to get her mind off her most recent preoccupations. She had no idea how long she would be without a vehicle, so her options were limited to say the least. She decided to take a closer look at some of the outbuildings she'd inventoried last week. That outing had led to the discovery of Lisette's little house, and Randi couldn't help but wonder what puzzles she might encounter today.

It was hard to know how to feel about everything now. The matter of her father's disappearance had been put to rest by Lavinia's admission of his abandonment, and now she would be making renovation decisions through the filter of a new set of emotions. Somehow, she didn't have the same enthusiasm for the project right now, but she wasn't convinced the feeling was anything more than temporary heartsickness. For now, she was grateful she wasn't under the gun to make any decisions today, and that fact gave her comfort as she set out down the lane that divided the farmyard.

All the outbuildings were situated behind the house, the first one set back about fifty feet from the back steps. There were several small buildings interspersed throughout the yard, but she had little recollection as to the function for most of the structures. She could recognize the hen house by the nesting trays and the remnants of the chicken wire enclosure. The smokehouse was recognizable because it was small and had no windows. Other than those two and the stable, the buildings yielded few clues as to their intended purpose. While most of the buildings appeared to be fairly sturdy, a couple seemed to be on their last legs. All of them had seen better days, and Randi was sorry the place had been allowed to fall into such disrepair.

The cotton ginning shed and equipment barn lay farther down the lane to her right, and she hurried down the path with memories exploding in her head. The ginning shed had been under construction at the time of her father's disappearance, which was another reason his abandonment seemed so impossible to comprehend. The building itself had been completed, and the equipment was expected to be delivered in time for fall harvest. She remembered how excited her father had been at the prospect of ginning his own cotton harvest, and he'd had high hopes that other area farmers would bring their crop to Willow Bend as well. Lavinia had pronounced the gin a colossal waste of good money and had never set foot in the place, as far as Randi knew. Her father had been gone for weeks by the time the machinery and equipment arrived, so it was returned to the factory without ever being unloaded from the delivery trucks.

Randi paused at the entrance, unsure if she wanted to brave the dreariness within. Though the building was open on each end, the desolation of the gloomy interior belied the bright sunshine that surrounded it. Sadness washed over her as she realized that the structure was a monument to dreams unrealized. This was the newest building on the farm, yet it looked no better for the wear than the others, groaning and decrepit in their neglect. She entered today, having limited herself to a quick glance through the entry bay during last week's explorations.

She walked down the center aisle of the shed tentatively, taking care not to stir up any critters that might be nesting in the leaves and trash that had blown in and piled up over the decades. She stopped about midway down the aisle, thinking about the cotton wagons that never came. Randi looked around at the disappointing reality of this newest building's fate, glad that her father wasn't here to see it in this sorry state. Junk and old furniture were piled to the rafters in every corner, and untidy piles of old tires and empty bottles littered the ground here and there. She looked back at the path before her, certain that forward motion should only continue with careful steps and a watchful eye. She finally made it to the other end of the shed, anxious to leave the gloom of this place behind her.

Her eyes were adjusting to the brilliance of the day when she spotted an ancient truck parked a short distance from the ginning shed. It seemed to be in an odd place, positioned not at the edge of the woods that lay beyond it, but parked haphazardly as if the driver had simply gotten out and left it where it stalled. She knew abandoned vehicles were a typical find on old farmsteads, but she hadn't noticed any others around Willow Bend. It was curious this one was out in the open like this. As she approached, Randi noticed the truck was loaded with bricks, the wheel rims flattened under the heavy load. She walked over and gingerly placed her foot on the running board, testing the integrity of the metal before trusting it with her weight. There was no give, so she heaved herself up and tried the driver's side door. It was either locked or jammed, and the windows were far to grimy to see anything within.

Randi stepped down and noted there was no clearance between the truck and the ground beneath, owing to years of debris that had blown under the rusting hulk. She was sure an abandoned vehicle was the haven of choice for rats, snakes and spiders, and she didn't plan to linger. This relic would have to be dragged off, and she made a mental note to ask Hitch for his suggestions the next time they met. Thoughts of Hitch brought fresh uneasiness to her conscience once again, and she told herself she would absolutely confess her omissions at the earliest opportunity. She turned her back on the ancient truck and refocused on her explorations. Unwilling to go back the way she came, she walked around the outside of the ginning shed and headed back down the lane.

The stable and paddock were closer to the house, and she was eager to revisit the place that evoked such fond memories. The stable had been home to her pony, and she'd spent many happy hours brushing and grooming her lustrous coat. Until now, Randi had only allowed herself the memory of the pony's soft whickering in her ear as she nuzzled her hair. Randi had nothing but time today, so she let the memories take her where they would. She closed her eyes and entered the barn slowly, counting off the thirteen steps from the entry door to the pony's stall, just as she'd done as a child. She opened her eyes when she bumped into the hinged gate after a count of twelve.

"Right stall, longer legs!", she said to some doves nesting in the rafters.

"Billie" had been the last Christmas gift she'd received from her daddy. Her mother had not approved of the pony, and Lavinia had been none too happy when her protests were overridden by Henry's enthusiasm for riding. He believed all proper young ladies were to be instructed in certain arts, and equestrian arts were high on his list. Randi and her father had ridden nearly every day after Billie's arrival, and he'd often told her mother that he preferred the company of his horse and his bird dog to almost anyone he knew. He'd talked to Beau and Buck as if they'd had good sense, and was not often seen around the farm without one or the other, or both. Lavinia had won in the end though, as the horses were the first things sold after he'd gone. Randi had cried for days after Billie was carted off to a nearby farm. She'd hated her mother for that single act above all others and had often thrown it up to her as an example of her heartlessness and cruelty.

Randi hadn't thought about the horses in years, and she wondered if the fresh wave of desolation she was feeling was due to the memory of the pony or the turmoil the visit with Lavinia had caused. After all, Randi did have a few good memories from the time she and her mother had spent on their own. It's true the relationship would probably have fared better without the succession of husbands and suitors, but Lavinia's disclosure about her husband's affair and subsequent abandonment had shed new light on that subject. Perhaps she could come to see her mother through new eyes in time, after she had a chance to get comfortable with a new point of view.

The sun was climbing higher in the sky and Randi decided to walk to the highway for the mail before it got any hotter. Evening thunderstorms were a given this time of year, and she'd likely have to spend some time holed up in the camper. She hoped her magazine subscriptions would catch up with her soon, as she was getting low on reading material. A trip to the library would be in order just as soon as she got her wheels back.

Randi was sorting through items marked "Occupant" and the latest no-name sweepstakes mailing when she came upon the letter addressed to "New Owner of Willow Bend".

———————

Hitch picked up his cell phone for the third time and put it back down. What he had to say really should be delivered in person. He'd already cancelled his other appointments, offering the best excuse he could come up with considering his mood. He really did feel sick to his stomach, but it didn't have anything to do with the quality of the food at the diner. His visit with Hal Crews had been enlightening to say the least, and now he felt disgusted with himself. He pulled out of the diner parking lot with every intention of sulking in the comfort of his own home, but the road ahead seemed to beckon him onward to Willow Bend.

CHAPTER TWELVE

Sounds of distant thunder roused Randi from her thoughts, and she turned up the radio just in time to hear the latest weather alert for the tri-county area. Though the kitchen window was small, she could see the angry thunderheads forming on the horizon, the graying conditions a perfect backdrop for her mood. Randi's emotions had run the gamut this afternoon, and now her surprise and excitement had been replaced by cold dread as she considered the implications of this new information.

The letter addressed to the "New Owner of Willow Bend" had been from Dr. Henriette Benson, a physician from upstate New York, who was seeking information from whoever now lived at the last known address for her father. Her letter stated she had little information other than his last known address, and she'd not seen him since moving north with her mother many years ago. The sister Randi had been ignorant of up until a few days ago had found her, and now she was faced with the stark fact that her mother had brazenly lied to her and sent her on her way. Obviously, Henry Moore had not taken Lisette and the child to Canada, as her mother said, and now she had to wonder why Lavinia had concocted such a tale.

Randi now realized the significance of the promise her mother required in exchange for her story. In good faith Randi had promised to never again bring up that painful chapter of their lives, and in return her mother had offered her nothing more than a story. Why would Lavinia say her husband had dumped them in favor of his other family if he hadn't? Her mother must have known that would be hurtful information, so why do it?

Randi kept going over the sparse details of the conversation with her mother, hoping to recall something that would exonerate her. Lavinia claimed she'd hired a private investigator who confirmed Henry Moore was living in Ontario with a wife and child, yet Henriette Benson's letter referenced an upbringing in New Jersey. Randi had even asked her mother if there had been any contact in the fifty years since he'd left, and she'd claimed there was a letter confirming his new life and offering an apology to his daughter. No, there was only one explanation, and Randi wiped away a solitary tear as she realized the enormity of her mother's willful deceit. It was bad enough to learn that her mother had lied all these years by letting her think her father had vanished without a trace. Now she'd claimed to know all the while that they'd been abandoned. Lavinia's claim that she'd kept the desertion secret to spare her daughter's feelings, rang hollow now, and Randi wished she'd never gone to Florida.

Try as she might, Randi couldn't stop wondering why her mother would tell such an elaborate lie. The letter of inquiry from Henriette Benson painted a picture that was clear enough. Even the name seemed to bear witness. Henry and Lisette easily translated to Henriette, and she'd lived at Willow Bend as a young child, over fifty years ago. She was the baby in the basket, and now that baby was reaching out with questions of her own. Lavinia's story was now just another piece of a dizzying puzzle, and Randi wondered yet again what purpose her mother's latest fabrication was meant to serve. Why would it suit Lavinia for Randi to believe her father had lived out his days in Canada with his other family? Why would such a lie be more palatable than the truth, assuming Lavinia knew the truth?

Randi was shaken back to reality by buffeting winds, and she threw open the door of the camper to assess the approaching storm. To her dismay, she saw that conditions outside were just as turbulent as her thoughts, and now she was in grave danger. She ran down the lane as fast as she could, wondering which of the sorry buildings would best provide safety.

She'd decided on the horse barn when she saw Hitch's truck speeding up the driveway. Randi reversed course and ran toward the truck, reaching it just as the bottom fell out. Hitch opened the door from the inside and she leaped into the cab with relief. Though panting from her exertions, she couldn't help but laugh as she realized Hitch had rescued her yet again. She was just about to thank him for his chivalry when she noticed his odd expression. The seconds dragged by under the intensity of his gaze, and the torrent of rain on the roof was no match for the heart pounding silence that filled the interior of the truck. Randi's stomach turned over as Hitch carefully enunciated every syllable of her given name.

"Hello, Miranda."

CHAPTER THIRTEEN

The sounds of the storm faded into the background and Randi was painfully aware of the silence between them. Hitch's demeanor was stony and stiff, and she knew she deserved the ill feelings harbored toward her. There was nothing to do but plunge into it headlong. She took a deep breath and forced an apology around the lump that seemed to stick in her throat.

"Hitch, I didn't mean to deceive you." Randi said with a ragged breath.

"And yet you did." he replied, without a hint of compassion.

"There just never seemed to be a good time. I liked you so much from the moment I met you, and we were getting along so well..." Her voice trailed off and she turned away to hide the tears that threatened to escape. She dared not lower her head, lest he see tears falling to her lap. Randi hadn't cried in front of anyone in years, and she blinked repeatedly, resisting the urge to wipe her face with her sleeve.

"Didn't it occur to you that your identity might be important information? I'll concede there was no reason to tell me when we first met, but how about later? How about last night?" Hitch's voice was very controlled, and to Randi, it was more frightening than if he'd launched into a bombastic fit.

"You let me go on and on about your family, and you never said a word. You let me talk about your mother...." Hitch's tone changed at the last, and he expelled a sigh of frustration. "I thought we were on our way to something. Guess I'm an asshole."

Randi spun toward him, tears streaming unheeded.

"Hitch, I hope we're on our way to something! These past few days have been the best I've had in years. Between my dad disappearing and Bill dying on me, I never expected to have anything left of my heart. But here you are, and I find that I might still be alive after all."

Now Hitch turned away. The rain ran down the windows in rivers and it was impossible to see anything beyond the glass. Randi slid across the seat, praying her advances wouldn't be unwelcome. In that moment she realized she would sacrifice any amount of pride to have this man's forgiveness. She threw her arms around him as best she could and pressed her face to his chest.

"I know it's a little late, but I planned to tell you as soon as I saw you again. Please say you'll forgive me and we can get past this. I wanted to say something last night, but your memories of my mother...." her voice trailed off at the last. "I was ashamed."

Randi sensed his body tensing beneath hers, and she retreated to her side of the cab. She felt humiliated, and she covered her mouth with one hand as she reached for the door handle with the other.

Hitch reached across to halt her exit and dragged her back toward him with a crushing embrace. He tilted her head back and began to cover her neck with kisses. Soon their hungry mouths found each other, and they held onto one another with an urgency that shook Randi down to her bones. They struggled with their clothes, both seeming to need the closeness, and his lips sought out her breasts as soon as they were unbound. She couldn't stifle the moan that escaped her lips, and Hitch returned his attention to her mouth in answer. A deafening clap of thunder accompanied their coupling, and Randi couldn't tell the lightning flashes from the light show that exploded in her brain as they reached their crescendo. They lay there in a tangled heap for a few precious minutes, neither speaking lest the moment be spoiled. The storm that had raged around them only minutes ago was now reduced to pattering rain and distant thunder, and the skies began to lighten.

Randi held onto him tightly, unwilling to let him go just yet. Even if Hitch's anger was as spent as the storm's fury, there would still be some explaining to do. It was hard to know where to begin, but she resolved he'd know as much as she did by the end of the day. Hitch seemed to be a man who valued truth, and if she had any hope of a relationship with him, she'd have to proceed on that footing from here on out.

They parted to straighten their clothes, and Randi wondered if she should be concerned about the continuing silence. Perhaps Hitch was still mad after all. Those thoughts lasted about two seconds.

"Man, I'm glad I opted for a bench seat when I ordered this last truck!" Hitch laughed. "I'm really getting too old for this sort of thing." His grin was quick and easy, and Randi joked that it had been awhile since she'd last had a tumble in a pickup.

She checked the buttons of her blouse for a third time as Hitch adjusted the wipers and swung the truck around toward the camper. Randi and Hitch both sat there for a few seconds, staring stupidly. Finally, their eyes were able to assimilate the scene before them. The camper had been parked under a mighty oak to take advantage of the shade provided by its magnificent spreading boughs. Apparently that last sharp crack of lightning had struck the tree and broken out the top section, hurling it onto the roof of the camper. The point of impact was nearly the center, and each end was bowed up like a giant horseshoe. Randi stared at the mess as fresh tears formed. She was homeless! Nearly everything she had, little as that was, had been in the camper. Hitch was the first to break the shocked silence that filled the truck's interior.

"I guess this means you'll be staying with me for a while."

CHAPTER FOURTEEN

R andi awoke from a dream that featured her mother's legs
sticking out from under the ruined camper, much like the
scene from the Wizard of Oz. She contemplated what Freud
would have to say about that as she headed for the bathroom of
Hitch's cabin. He had played the role of hero once again, fishing
her essentials out of the crushed camper and covering the wreck
with tarps to prevent any further water damage to what was left of
her possessions. Randi's homeless status had been revoked almost
immediately by his offer of the cabin until renovations could render
at least a portion of Willow Bend livable. His assurance that her
presence would cause him no inconvenience was accompanied by a
wink and a promise to drop by frequently to catch a fish or two, and
Bo had promptly been dispatched for guard duty.

Randi had intended to share her story in full detail, but Hitch
had insisted after a couple of sentences that the day had been trying enough without a rehash. Somehow, he seemed to realize that

Randi needed time to come to terms with her former life and her mother's lies, and he was offering to be a patient participant in the process. She smiled to herself as she thought about how lucky she was to have stumbled across such a good man. Second chances were rare, especially for someone her age, and she couldn't help but feel she had a very good chance, right within her grasp. There hadn't been a serious love interest either before or since Bill, and she felt a slight pang of guilt to know she was thinking of him less and less these days. Hitch Williams seemed like a good gamble, based on what she knew of him so far, and she prayed her growing feelings were not misplaced.

She combed her hair, brushed her teeth and applied minimal makeup. After all, she couldn't go anywhere without any wheels, and it didn't appear that Bo would mind if she made a casual Friday out of a Tuesday. She was lucky to have her personal grooming items at all, and she was thankful she hadn't yet unpacked her case from the weekend. Happily, the overnight bag had slid toward the only point of accessibility of the wrecked camper, and Hitch had been able to slip it out through what was left of the door. She was still missing her purse, but she was hopeful to be reunited with it at Hitch's earliest convenience. For now, she had some homework to do, as Hitch had left cost estimates and preliminary drawings for her review. That would keep her busy for a while, and she left the bathroom satisfied with her reflection.

As she considered her options among the meager wardrobe assembled in the bedroom closet, Randi thought about the whirlwind her life had been these past several days. It seemed incomprehensible that she'd learned of Lisette's existence just last week.

A day later she'd confronted her mother and learned the scope of Lavinia's deception. By the wee hours of the next morning she'd embarked on an affair with a man she hardly knew, and by Sunday night she was riddled with remorse for perpetuating her own lie of omission. Yesterday she'd learned her half-sister was alive and well and looking for answers, just as she was. The fact that all her worldly possessions were now in a heap inside the twisted metal frame of her former home seemed a fitting topper, and she said another prayer of thanks that she hadn't been inside to share the fate of her things. All in all, it had been the most unsettling several days of her life, and Randi hoped she wouldn't be treated to quite so much excitement any time soon.

Randi found a pair of old sweatpants with a drawstring waist and pulled them on. They were way too long, but fortunately the elastic at the bottom of the legs allowed the excess fabric to bunch up at the ankles. There were three shirts hanging on the rod and she chose the least offensive color and pattern available. She could see why these items had been relegated to the fish camp and was disappointed to realize this was all she'd have to wear when Hitch returned this evening. She was ruefully aware that Hitch had yet to see her at her best, and by now he may be wondering if it got any better than what he'd seen so far. She just had to get her wheels back! Reliable transportation and cell service hadn't seemed like priorities in the face of her latest disaster with the camper, but now she was beginning to miss the necessities of life. If Hitch's friend couldn't fix her truck, she'd have to replace it immediately. She rummaged around the kitchen drawers for paper and pen to make a list. In addition to the obvious priority of follow-up with Henriette, there would be the matter of replacing the items required to lead a normal life.

Finding nothing of help in the kitchen, Randi walked over to an old roll top desk situated near the fireplace. The top was rolled down and did not yield to the gentle upward pressure she applied. The drawers were hard to pull out and groaned in protest, but the contents were hardly worth the effort required. The smaller drawer was filled with ancient decks of playing cards, poker chips and a lone pencil with a broken tip. A larger drawer contained some musty books on various topics and a rusty metal tackle box. She was rapidly losing hope of finding any writing materials when she came to the last drawer. To her delight there were several blank note pads situated right on top, with a header that read "Pinkney, Bowers & Crews Law Firm". She picked up the stack and counted four in all, apparently untouched since the sticky stripping at the top appeared to be pristine. The paper was slightly yellowed, and the print harkened back to another time. Randi felt some guilt about tearing off a page for personal use, but reasoned the pads were probably long forgotten anyway. As she placed the items back in the drawer she noticed a series of large manila envelopes in the bottom. They were envelopes of old photos, as she soon discovered, and Randi could hardly contain her excitement when she came across an envelope marked "Willow Bend".

———————

Hitch was pretty sure nothing could top yesterday's emotional roller coaster, but the anger he'd felt toward Randi had settled into a measure of empathy regarding her omission. She'd seemed genuinely contrite for keeping her identity a secret, and looking back, it was easy to see why she'd been reluctant to confess early on. He was hopeful he'd learn more about her tonight, now that she felt safe and things were out in the open.

Henry Moore's daughter had quite a history and some emotional baggage from the sound of it, but who didn't? Randi couldn't be blamed for her mother's bitchiness any more than he could be blamed for his father's drunkenness. Hitch was hopeful that ancient history could be put in its proper place eventually, but he had a feeling it was going to take some patience and effort to get there. Women! Who was he trying to kid? He was tickled pink to be dealing with female intrigue and entanglements of the heart. It had been a long time since he'd had to deal with a woman's needs or feelings. He laughed to himself as he realized he hadn't felt this alive in years.

CHAPTER FIFTEEN

The black and white photos had captured life as she'd known it at Willow Bend and Randi couldn't believe her good fortune. Someone, most likely Hitch, had managed to preserve in pictures so many scenes that lived only in her memory. There was a picture of Henry Moore on his horse, and another of him posing with a great buck he'd killed on a hunt. There were pictures of hired men working on the farm, and one of her father's prize coon dog. Randi lingered over the pictures, drinking in the memories as they washed over her. There was a picture of the house and another of the completed ginning shed. Her father was posing in front of his grand construction project, grinning from ear to ear. Her heart skipped a beat as she realized the photo must have been taken within weeks of his disappearance from her life. Could he really have been standing there smiling so proudly if he was preparing to abandon his family? She searched his handsome face for an answer. No, she'd never believe it. Everything Randi remembered about her father told her it couldn't be true, and indeed Henriette's letter seemed to support an alternate version of events.

Yellowed newspaper clippings were in the same envelope, and her heart raced as she read the printed details that appeared in the local weekly. "Information Sought on Missing Man" and "Moore Disappearance Probed" were extensive articles, each giving a narrative of the known facts. Both referenced a statement from the sheriff indicating that foul play could be involved, and various leads were being investigated. Randi read and reread each word, convinced she would glean some fresh nuance that could shed light on the truth. The trouble was, with all the information and misinformation she'd been given, would she recognize the truth if she ever found it? Randi continued to leaf through the contents of the envelope, the last article titled "New Clues in Moore Case". The piece reported that an unnamed source had positively identified the remains of Henry Moore's hunting dog on property adjacent to Willow Bend, but it went on to say that the importance of this was unclear since there was conflicting information about when the dog was last seen in the company of his owner.

As Randi was returning the articles and photos, she realized there was an additional item hung in the bent corner of the envelope. She drew out a small, yellowed envelope with no markings. It was sealed, and Randi was ashamed by how little hesitation she felt as she opened it. The pictures and newspaper clippings had been an unexpected find, and she could scarcely believe her innocent snooping had yielded such a treasure trove of information. The fact that she'd rummaged through Hitch's personal possessions was something she'd contemplate later, but right now there was no force of man or nature that would deter her from discovering the contents of this last envelope. Randi pulled out the single black and white photo with a shaking hand.

Though the shot wasn't as clear as the others and her back was turned to the camera, there was no mistaking the woman in the photo. Even if Randi hadn't recognized her mother's distinctive hairstyle, she would have recognized the dress. Her father had often remarked that it was his favorite, and Lavinia had worn it the day they drove to Charleston to tell Randi's grandparents their son was missing. While it was easy enough to identify Lavinia in the photo, the man was a stranger. Lavinia had her arms around his neck and was obviously saying something the man found amusing. A stolen moment had been captured on film, but who had taken the photo? Hitch? It was obviously taken with the same camera and fit the time frame. Did Hitch know the man in the photo? As she contemplated that possibility, his contempt for her mother became clear. Did he know something she'd been unaware of all these years? Had Lavinia been carrying on with another man while living at Willow Bend? The prospect of an affair added another dimension to the tawdry tale, and Randi felt sick at the thought of it all.

Her mind raced back to the recollections Hitch had shared on Sunday night. His memories of Henry Moore had been warm and positive. On the other hand, the remarks about her mother seemed anything but complimentary. What did Hitch know, and how much had he understood back then as a twelve-year-old boy? Did he know about her father's affair with Lisette? Did he know about the baby? And if he did, why did he consider her father less disreputable than her mother? It didn't make sense. Hitch had obviously admired Henry Moore, but had nothing good to say about his wife. His impression had been shaped by more than the rudeness Lavinia had displayed on the porch of Willow Bend, that much Randi was sure of.

A cold lump replaced Randi's excitement as she realized she'd see Hitch again in a matter of hours. These revelations about her family had come about as a result of plundering his desk. While her motives had been innocent enough initially, she couldn't help but wonder how all of this would look to him. Would he believe she'd been searching for no more than paper and pen when she stumbled across the articles and photos? Would her reasons even matter? They already had a lot to overcome, and she'd let her curiosity overrule good manners. Well, it was done now, and she couldn't undo it. Sure, she'd have to apologize, but she wasn't about to let propriety or conscience deter her from her questions. She'd have to take whatever was coming to her in exchange for answers. She resolved she wouldn't be the only one confessing tonight. Hitch Williams would have to spill everything he ever knew about Willow Bend, the Moore family, and the mystery man in the photo.

CHAPTER SIXTEEN

They'd had a wonderful dinner, but Randi had been too distracted to enjoy it. Hitch had noticed, and Randi felt bad about the way the evening had gone so far. He'd arrived at the cabin with a shopping bag and an invitation to dine in town, promising they'd have plenty of time to talk later. The dress he'd selected for her was a simple red cotton fabric featuring scattered daisies, and the scoop neckline and tie back waist made for a flattering fit. She'd been impressed by his guesswork, and he'd confessed that her build was nearly the same as his late wife. He'd seemed sheepish at the admission, and Randi had assured him the gift was much appreciated. She was glad she hadn't lost her sandals as she ran from the camper, as Hitch hadn't thought of that. The few articles of clothing she owned at this point would need to be recycled very soon, and Randi made a mental note to ask about using a washer and dryer once they got past the inevitable round of truth and consequences.

Dinner had been accompanied by small talk and Hitch's narrative on who was who as the locals filed in for sustenance. He included the latest gossip on the buxom waitress who took their order and Randi was reminded of the perils of small-town life. Several people looked their way over dinner, and there was no doubt that she and Hitch were providing fresh fodder for the Baptists and the gossips. Hitch had already admitted that her identity had been revealed by the town lawyer, who just happened to be a childhood friend. It seemed Hal Crews remembered that Henry and Lavinia Moore had a daughter, and a new client named Miranda M. Jackson seemed to be just about the right age. It hadn't taken much digging for Hal to confirm it was no coincidence, and Hitch had been the second to know. Randi wondered if there might be an ethical issue attached to the disclosure, but decided it wasn't worth the effort to consider. While the method and timing of the revelation hadn't been ideal, it was a relief to have things out in the open.

Hitch was on his way back from the men's room, and the buxom waitress had brought the change in his absence. Weighty subjects would be their dessert, and Randi couldn't help but feel anxious about the evening ahead. Part of her wanted to forget everything about her past and concentrate on the possibilities for the future, but another part of her longed to know the truth at any cost. Randi was certain she'd be unable to move forward until she was satisfied she'd done all she could to resolve the lingering questions surrounding her father's disappearance, and Hitch would be an integral part of that journey. She would deal with Henriette's questions and Lavinia's deceptions later. Right now her concern was how things would play out tonight.

Hitch angled toward the table and favored her with one of his charming smiles. Randi prayed a silent prayer that he'd still be smiling later. He'd been hurt and disappointed yesterday, and she was afraid her latest transgression would add insult to injury. He scooped up the change and counted out a generous tip for the infamous waitress before they headed for the door. While Hitch seemed anxious to get back to the cabin, Randi wasn't so sure.

"By the way, I spoke with the repair shop late this afternoon." Hitch reported affably. "My buddy thinks he can have the new alternator on it by Friday. Had to order it, you know. Parts for something that old aren't exactly stock items."

Hitch's teasing tone began to put her at ease, and she willed herself to lighten up, at least until they got back to the cabin.

"It's likely the parts cost more than the truck's worth. I might have to let him keep it." Randi quipped. "How old of a guy is your buddy? It occurs to me that I might have to offer a trade." she said with a wink. "My credit card is somewhere in the camper."

"You know, you bring up a good point, Randi. In fact, I've just realized what a position I'm in here." Hitch replied, opening the truck door with one hand and guiding her toward the seat with the other. His facial expression was quite serious, and Randi wondered where this discussion was going as he stepped around to the driver's side. She didn't have to wonder any longer than it took to slam the door.

"No purse, no cash, no credit card, no ID, no cell phone..." he leaned into her space, doing his best attempt at a lecherous smile. "It's not like you can go anywhere. Guess that makes you my prisoner."

The giggle died on her lips as he swept her up into a crushing embrace and kissed her soundly. The teasing was quickly turning into something else, and Randi felt the familiar heat he'd so recently reignited. The fact they were in a parking lot and it was still daylight was slow to dawn on them both, but decorum finally won out. They felt like a couple of teenagers caught parking and Hitch even barked a tire as they turned onto the highway. She giggled as he plugged in a radar detector and made a big show of stomping on the gas. It didn't appear Hitch had conversation on his mind, and Randi had to admit that she was feeling less than focused on anything other than the ten or twelve steps it would take them from the front door to the bedroom. Maybe it would do them good to take a little personal time before they discussed more troubling issues. Maybe some good old-fashioned physical exertion would soften the edges of such heavy topics. Maybe what lay in the past wasn't nearly as important as what was here, right now. Hitch must have been thinking along the same lines. They were back at the cabin in less than ten minutes.

Hitch got out of the truck and hustled around to the passenger side to give Randi the red-carpet treatment. He'd thought about a hotel, but that would require a trip to another town. It also had an air of impropriety to it that just didn't fit. What was going on between them wasn't tawdry or inappropriate. He'd been thinking about her practically every minute since he'd left her alone with her thoughts last night. He knew she felt bad about deceiving him, and that was a good sign, wasn't it? She'd seemed contrite and eager to have his forgiveness, and he was happy to give it. A walk down memory lane wasn't always a good thing, and he much preferred thinking about what might be ahead to what was already behind. Right now, he intended to deal with his more urgent needs, especially since Randi seemed to be like-minded for the moment. There would be plenty of time to talk later.

CHAPTER SEVENTEEN

Randi had expected to wake up this morning with more answers than questions, but it wasn't to be. She and Hitch had talked most of the night, and yet she didn't feel any closer to the finish line. Their passionate interlude had indeed softened the platform for their discussions, and they'd ended up with a joint resolution to get to the bottom of the mystery of her father's disappearance once and for all. Though Randi had been confounded to learn her mother's deceptions were far more extensive than she imagined, she was heartened to know that Hitch was as committed to answers as she was. They even had a game plan in place, and they had a list of resources to help put it all together. As luck would have it, Hitch's calendar would be dedicated to Willow Bend for the next several weeks, and they hoped to accomplish more than renovations during that time.

For now, Randi had been charged with the task of compiling the notes they made last night. The pictures and articles from the desk drawer were organized into a timeline that spread across the kitchen table. Hitch was certain that between the two of them, some long-forgotten clue would surface and a working theory would emerge. He'd attacked the problem from a project management point of view, and Randi could easily see why he'd won awards for some of his renovation work. Somehow, having a partner in all of this made it more bearable, and Randi had been relieved beyond words that Hitch harbored no ill will over the snooping that led to the discovery of the photos. He'd joked that he expected nothing less from a nosey woman, and she conceded she'd earned the stereotype.

Randi decided to concentrate her notes on Hitch's recollections first, especially since her own were of little use thus far. He remembered taking part in the search party that was organized after Mrs. Moore raised the alarm. In fact, Hitch and his father had been questioned by the sheriff as part of the investigation. Everyone at Willow Bend had been questioned about the last time they saw Henry Moore, and an accident somewhere on the property was eventually floated as a plausible theory. A search party had been formed to rule that out, and as far as Hitch knew, all 7,000 acres had been scoured over a period of several days. Henry Moore had not been on his horse at the time, that much they knew, but it was Hitch that pointed out the dog was missing as well. The hound's remains were found some months later, on an adjacent plantation, identified by the collar and tags issued by the local veterinarian. Most of this information was verified by the articles she'd already read, but Hitch had been able to supply Randi with a detail the sheriff never got. Hitch had indeed taken the photograph of her mother and the mystery man, just days before Henry Moore was officially reported missing. This tidbit had been withheld for good reason. The man with his arms around Lavinia Moore was Twig Williams, Hitch's father.

Hitch had felt the need to offer a disclaimer once he'd identified the man in the photo. He swore that as far as he knew, prior to that day, Lavinia had never spoken to, much less touched Twig Williams. In fact, as he recalled, contact with Lavinia Moore was never a pleasant experience for the hired help, as she made little attempt to conceal her disdain for her husband's minions. Hitch had been shocked to see such a display of affection between them, and he could only blame his fascination with detective magazines for taking the photo in the first place. He was terrified it would be discovered and he'd be punished, and he'd waited several years to have the film developed. Even then he'd had the photographs developed in another town, just in case someone could recognize his father. He'd kept the photos hidden away all these years, the damning one separate from the rest.

Hitch had also provided Randi with a history lesson on Willow Bend. He'd already told her the property had been a Williams family holding before the War Between the States. She'd learned last night that Colonel Jesson Williams' plantation had been confiscated in retaliation for a successful raid he'd led against a Union supply depot early in the hostilities. The Colonel had died in a field hospital from wounds sustained in one of the final skirmishes in Virginia, and the surviving family members had been evicted promptly at war's end. The property was held by a series of owners through the end of the century, during which time the original plantation home burned. A railroad executive from New York had purchased Willow

Bend by 1900, and the present house had been constructed about 1905.

Henry Moore's father had purchased it all on a tax sale back in the 1940s but had long since moved his ailing wife to Charleston by the time of Randi's birth. Hitch's father had harbored more than a passing bitterness about the reversal of fortunes his family had suffered, and he'd always hoped to regain the birthright that had been stripped from his great-great grandfather. T.G. "Twig" Williams had all hope dashed when Henry Moore rolled in from college to assume operation of the farm, and further insult had been added when Twig found himself accepting wages from the young owner some years later. The disappointments of life had finally proved too much for Hitch's father, and his frequent drinking had progressed to full blown alcoholism by the late sixties. Twig died in 1972 after a long battle with the bottle, bitter until the very end about the injustices of life and the other demons that plagued him. Just what those other demons were, Hitch never knew, and he'd never shared the photo or its implications with another living soul until now.

As interesting as the Williams family history lesson had been, the most important information had been revealed when Randi told Hitch about the letter from Henriette. Randi picked up the damning photograph and looked at it again. What else could she conclude from the embrace nobody else was supposed to see? Her mother was an undisputed liar, and possibly a cheat if the photo was admitted as evidence. What was Lavinia up to with the deceptive tale she'd offered her trusting daughter? Lavinia had asserted her husband left them for Lisette and their child, as if there wasn't a single doubt in her mind. Henriette's letter said she was inquiring at the last known address for her father, and that much was true. A lot of people lived on Willow Bend in those days, including Hitch's family. Henriette's name seemed to bear witness to her lineage, but Lavinia had offered the ultimate lie. Henriette wasn't Randi's half-sister, as her mother had asserted. Lisette's child had been fathered by Twig Williams, and everyone at Willow Bend knew it.

———————

Hitch hadn't let on to Randi, but he'd hardly slept. He'd relocated to the kitchen after a few hours of restlessness, hoping a magazine would clear out the troubling memories that churned in his mind. He'd never required much sleep, but he did value peace of mind. It had taken a good portion of his adult life to stop thinking about those days, and here he was reliving 1965 all over again. Sure, he wanted to help Randi find answers, but at what cost? It wasn't likely they'd ever learn what happened to her father, and then what? Would she be stuck on it, never able to move forward with her life?

Yes, it had been a bad chapter for Randi, and the worst episode of his own young life had happened just days before Henry Moore's disappearance was announced. He'd come upon his father parking a brand new farm truck over by the ginning shed, positioning it just so. Then he'd watched incredulously as Twig ripped out some wires and removed something from the engine. Hitch had stopped dead in his tracks, but Twig had caught sight of his son just about the time he slammed down the hood. Hitch turned to run, but his father caught up with him a short distance from the woods. Without a word of explanation, Twig had given his son the beating of his life, promising to give him another if he ever ran his mouth about things that weren't his business. Life was never the same after that day, and his father's drinking had gone from bad to worse.

That had been Hitch's last summer at Willow Bend. He'd eventually escaped Twig's drunken ravings by moving to town to live with his sister and brother in law. He'd joined the army as soon as he was old enough to put South Carolina and Willow Bend behind him. He'd applied himself to an education, honed his craft over a period of years, and saved enough to start his own business. He'd come home and done just that, making a life, and loving a family along the way. Hitch had never been one to dwell on the past, and he wasn't about to get bogged down today. Even though he'd loved and lost, he was hopeful to love again. He'd get Randi pointed forward somehow, and his confidence in his ability to do that would have to be comfort enough for now. Hitch put the truck in park, downed the last of his coffee, and grabbed the list for the building supply store.

CHAPTER EIGHTEEN

Where the heck was Hitch? A quarter hour had passed since he'd taken off down the lane like a mad man. He'd only broken stride long enough to turn back and shout that she should wait for him. Now she was leaning against a sorry-looking fence near the ginning shed, wondering what was going to happen next.

The last few days had seen a flurry of activity at Willow Bend, and in fact this evening had been the first down time they'd had since the storm damage. Hitch already had a crew assigned to the camper cleanup, and he hoped to be ready to start on the house renovations within the week. Randi had been reunited with her truck in the interim and had set out on her errands almost immediately. The first day had been consumed with restoring order to the items salvaged from the ruined camper and replacing the items that hadn't survived. A cute boutique in town had yielded a few nice additions to what remained of her wardrobe, and a cell dealer in the neighboring town had upgraded her to a new phone. The second day had been spent sifting through small items and papers that were unfortunately mixed in with the contents of the camper's only trash can. The letter from Henriette had been retrieved after considerable effort, and Randi had put in a call to her messaging service yesterday evening. Henriette was expected to return from an overseas trip by week's end, and Randi was hopeful she'd hear from her soon.

Randi had lots of questions to be sure, but only one thing needed verification at this point. Hitch had told her it was common knowledge that Twig was the father of Lisette's child, and yet they'd found something last night that had cast doubt on that claim. Hitch had surprised her once again with the admission that his late wife had been the daughter of the town lawyer from back in the day, and the old gentleman had lived to the ripe old age of ninety, retiring some twenty years previous. Upon his death, his Victorian home in the center of town passed to his deceased daughter's family, and Hitch had been living there for several years. He knew there were files in the attic, and it didn't take a rocket scientist to reason that Henry Moore had surely been a client. They'd gone up after dinner last night, agreeing that a cursory look couldn't hurt. Just as they were about to give up, Hitch had pulled out a file labeled "Unexecuted". About halfway through the pages, a single sheet bearing her father's name caught Randi's eye. The notes, written in the attorney's own hand, outlined his client's wishes that a codicil be added to his will, making provision for the financial support of Henriette, the minor child of Lisette Lewis. Hitch and Randi had both been stunned at the implication, and even more so when they realized the significance of the date scrawled at the top of the page. July 10th, 1965 couldn't have been more than a week or two before her father's disappearance. Had the document ever been prepared? Was it unexecuted because her father changed his mind, or because he disappeared before it got that far?

In light of last night's discovery, Randi had to wonder if her mother was telling the truth after all. If Henry Moore hadn't fathered Henriette, as Hitch insisted, why had he felt compelled to alter his financial affairs in such a way? Was Henriette really her sister, just as Lavinia had said? Hitch certainly doubted the possibility. While he would have been a much younger child at the time of Henriette's birth, he knew he'd never seen any evidence that Henry Moore ever visited Lisette's home, not even once. On the other hand, he'd frequently seen evidence of his father's visits. Hitch had always been the one to make any mail or grocery deliveries to Lisette, per Henry Moore's instructions, and he'd seen his dad leaving out the back door on more than one occasion. Hitch had always been careful to hang back along the tree line, giving his father ample time to clear out unseen. Twig had a volatile temper even without the bolstering effects of alcohol, and his son had learned early on that even a chance confrontation was best avoided.

Randi was roused from her thoughts by sounds of heavy equipment coming her way. Hitch was driving a bulldozer, and a burly, black man she'd met earlier in the day was following close behind on a small excavator. The cleanup crew had been wrapping up operations just about the time Hitch and Randi had set out on their walk, but now it appeared they had been diverted for another mission. Randi had been rattling on and pointing to the old truck with dry-rotted tires and a load of bricks, asking Hitch how they would move such a thing from the property. He'd stopped dead in his tracks, staring at it intently for just a few moments before he'd started back up the lane at a trot. Now Hitch was back and motioning to her to move away. He attached a hefty chain to the great rusted hitch on the back of the truck and got back on the bulldozer.

A mighty groan accompanied the progress of the hulking metal as Hitch dragged the truck from its resting place. A cloud of dust and grass rose up from its displacement and wafted toward Randi on a gentle breeze. She relocated to a vantage point near the tree line as Hitch settled on a stopping place and parked the dozer. Once the dust settled, the excavator moved in and began taking timid bites from the exposed soil. Randi's heart began to pound as she realized Hitch must be looking for something. At one point, the digging got too aggressive, and Hitch motioned for the operator to back off a bit. Minutes later, with her ears ringing from the cacophony of the equipment, she watched Hitch motion for the operator to stop and cut the engine. He disappeared from her sight for only a moment and reappeared with an ashen expression. He walked toward her slowly, his gaze locking with hers.

"Randi, I'm gonna need you to call 9-1-1 and ask the sheriff and coroner to come out to Willow Bend." Hitch dropped his head down and took a ragged breath before facing her again. "God help me, honey, I think I just found your father."

CHAPTER NINETEEN

They had driven all night, but now Hitch and Randi were parked in front of her mother's condo waiting for the sun to come up. The events of the last 48 hours seemed incredible to her, and Randi wondered if normal was a word that would ever again be associated with her life. She watched Hitch as he catnapped peacefully behind the wheel. She was glad he could sleep. She had yet to do so, and knew it was only adrenaline that kept her awake for now. The sooner she could see her mother, the better off she'd be. Not that she expected anything productive to come of it. Randi was braced for another regurgitation of lies, although she did wonder how even Lavinia could explain how a man who was supposed to be in Canada ended up in an old well in South Carolina.

Of course, the coroner had been quick to point out that identification was purely speculative at this point, but the DNA Randi had provided would clear up any doubt soon enough. Had their discovery been pure luck, or inevitable? There was no way to know. Something had gone off in Hitch's head the moment he saw the truck parked oddly near the corner of the ginning shed. He'd remembered that it was Twig who had placed it there, just so. The photo of Lavinia and Twig had been taken just a day or two after that.

Hitch had spent the better part of the last 48 hours berating himself for his failure to connect the dots sooner. Randi reminded him that a twelve-year-old boy could hardly be expected to contemplate such a possibility, and it was best not to speculate about what more could have been done fifty years ago. For now, Randi's intention was to offer Lavinia an opportunity to explain herself, and she hoped to use the threat of a renewed investigation to her advantage.

She checked her watch for the tenth time in as many minutes and resolved that seven am would be the hour of Lavinia's interrogation. Just a few minutes remained until the appointed hour, and Randi fought a faint feeling of nausea as she collected herself for the confrontation. Bless Hitch. He had offered to accompany her into the lion's den, but she'd assured him that driving her to Ft. Lauderdale was sacrifice enough. Randi intended to have a long-overdue one-on-one with her mother, and it was enough to know he was just outside if she needed him. She leaned over to kiss his rough, unshaven cheek, rousing him to wakefulness. They didn't speak, but he patted her hand and gave her a reassuring smile that said everything would be okay.

Trepidation gnawed at Randi as she made her way to her mother's door. Would she get any answers today, or would Lavinia offer yet another version of the truth? Randi was angry with her mother for her ongoing lies, but did she really believe her capable of murdering her husband and stuffing him down a well? Did her mother have help, as Hitch suggested? Did Twig do the dirty work and hide Henry away at Lavinia's request, in return for the promise of her favor? And what if her mother confessed? Was Randi prepared to see her mother go to prison? There were still so many questions, and the possibilities were all ugly.

Randi rang the doorbell three times, feeling not the slightest pang of guilt for the ambush she'd set for her Lavinia. She'd called her mother's number from a land line last night, just to make sure she was there. It had seemed cowardly to hang up after Lavinia answered, but Randi reminded herself that her mother could easily disappear if she felt cornered. Randi brushed her hair out of her face and set her jaw firmly as she heard the deadbolt turn. Expecting to see her mother disheveled and still in her pajamas, she was quite taken aback to see her mother fully dressed, with suitcases stacked neatly in the foyer. Lavinia seemed just as surprised to see her.

"Miranda, what on earth are you doing here at this ghastly hour of the morning?" Lavinia shook her head disapprovingly. "You should have called to tell me you were coming. I'm just this minute on my way out."

"Hello to you too, Mother." Randi said, glancing at the suitcases that suggested her mother had travel plans. "Aren't you going to invite me in?"

"Really, Miranda, I'm in quite a bit of a hurry. I'm expecting Manuel any moment." She craned her neck past her daughter and searched the street, rather nervously, Randi thought.

"Manuel?" Randi questioned?

"I told you about him. The golf pro I've been seeing for some months now. He has a condo in Spain, and I thought to spend the balance of the summer with him. It's so dreadfully hot here, you know." Lavinia reached back for the smallest case, bringing it forward in an effort to shepherd her daughter back toward the sidewalk.

Warning bells went off in Randi's head as it sank in that Lavinia was preparing to leave the country. Could she be imagining this perfect timing? Randi decided to play it cool for the moment.

"Yes, well good for you, Mother. I hope you and Manuel have a wonderful time. Before you go though, I do have a few more questions about your husband's disappearance." Randi crossed over the threshold, forcing her mother back into the foyer. She closed the door behind them and continued backing her mother toward the living room.

"I don't know what you mean, Miranda. I was very specific with you about your father's whereabouts, as well as the reasons for it. What else do you want from me? If you have other questions, perhaps you should contact the authorities in Canada and leave me alone." Lavinia's voice cracked a bit at the last, and Randi was certain she saw a flash of fear in her mother's eyes.

"I have contacted the authorities, Mother, but not the authorities in Canada." Randi's voice was flat calm, her eyes looking straight into her mother's.

Lavinia never looked away.

"You obviously think you know something, so just save me the trouble of guessing, Miranda. Unlike you, I have better things to do than dredge up the past."

The dig was meant to insult and divert, but Randi wasn't about to fall for it. She would have the answers she sought, once and for all, no matter how ugly it had to get.

"Fine." Randi continued. "I'll stick with what I know for now, then we can move on to what I suspect. I know everything you told me the last time I saw you is false. I know my father intended to alter his will to provide for Lisette's child, even though she was likely fathered by another man. I know that in the days following Daddy's disappearance from our lives, you had some kind of flirtation, if not an affair, with a man named Twig Williams. Most importantly, I know my father's remains were just removed from an old well at Willow Bend."

Lavinia's expression remained unchanged, and no denials or wails of protest were offered.

"Shall we move on to what I suspect?" Randi continued. "Did you kill him Mother, or did you get Twig to do it for you?"

"Everything I did was to protect you." Lavinia sighed, as if feigning patience with a small child. "You know I would not have gone to such lengths without a good reason."

Randi almost swallowed her tongue. She'd expected rebuttals from her mother, not admissions. She kept her voice calm, realizing anything threatening could bring about a sudden change of demeanor. Lavinia wanted to talk, so she would let her.

"What are you talking about, Mother? What did you do to protect me? Protect me from what?" This was a curve ball, and Randi was anxious to see where it would lead.

"You want to know how he ended up in that hole? We quarreled for the fiftieth time about that damn, bastard child. He wanted to provide for that gal and her child. There wasn't no reason for it. None!"

Randi was struck by the double negative and a change in her mother's voice. The woman speaking now was someone Randi didn't recognize. The accent was heavy, the words unpolished and unedited. This was a very different Lavinia.

"Wasn't the talk around town bad enough? Everyone knew that child's daddy was a white man. If Henry had his way, the whole town would have thought it was his. He didn't care a lick about that, but I did!"

Lavinia was as agitated as Randi had ever seen her, and the words tumbled out as if her mother had forgotten herself entirely. Randi listened in horrified fascination as the story continued.

"To hell with his reputation, but what about mine? What about yours? I wasn't gonna have it."

Lavinia took a breath, and Randi felt compelled to offer something to the dialog.

"Daddy wasn't unfaithful to you, Mama. Twig Williams fathered Lisette's child, not Daddy." Randi softened her tone, shocked by her mother's inexplicable transformation.

Lavinia looked at her daughter incredulously and continued.

"I knew that, but who else was gonna believe that? By the time Betty Taylor got through tellin' her tale all over town, what would it matter?"

"Betty Taylor?" Randi was confused. "Who is Betty Taylor?"

Lavinia stared at her daughter again, as if she were the one behaving oddly, and for a moment Randi wondered if her mother was having some kind of medical episode.

"Betty Taylor, Miranda. You know! The lawyer's secretary. You must remember her. She was my very best friend!"

It was Randi's turn to stare in disbelief.

"She had the biggest mouth in town!" Lavinia ranted. "If Betty had gotten the chance to tell one single person that Henry Moore was leavin' money for that woman and her bastard child, why tongues would have wagged for years. He'd just as well have worn a sign around his neck! So what if the child was Twig's? It wouldn't have mattered to a soul. He was no-count anyway. But Henry Moore? Now there's a story! So, he fell in a hole, we covered it up, and that was that!"

CHAPTER TWENTY

t had been weeks since Lavinia's disclosure that she'd known where her husband was all along. She claimed they'd been quarreling near the new ginning shed when he'd suddenly started sinking into the ground. He'd cried out only once and then disappeared, right before her mother's eyes. Hitch and his father had long believed the Williams' plantation home had been in that vicinity, and it was easy enough to deduce that an old well site had been compromised over the course of the land clearing activities. Lavinia had vehemently denied that she or Twig had done anything to her husband, but she readily admitted she'd seized upon the opportunity presented by the accident.

It had been easy enough to get Twig to go along with the plan after he'd come upon Lavinia peering down into the hole, especially after they couldn't get an answer to their calls. Twig had covered the hole with a couple of hay bales and set the truck over it, convincing the sheriff that the bricks were for an unfinished masonry job in connection with the new structure. The dog had been poisoned to keep him from calling attention to the area, and the other farm hands were too preoccupied with the search for their boss once the disappearance was announced. Nobody had paid a bit of attention to the oddly placed truck, and the search parties had focused their efforts on the wooded areas of Willow Bend over the next several weeks. Randi hadn't asked her mother what she'd promised Twig in exchange for his loyalty, but she had every idea their sudden departure from Willow Bend was fueled by mounting pressure to collect on the debt.

Randi didn't know where her mother was now. She'd walked out of the condo with her mother's feeble attempts at justification ringing in her ears. Lavinia's claims that all had been done to protect Randi from a social scandal and a ruined future seemed petty to say the least, and Randi was sick to her stomach to know her mother had used her to justify five decades of deceit. Even after her mother confessed all, she didn't seem to recognize she'd done anything wrong. She'd ticked off the details as if it was somebody else's life, never apologizing for robbing a child of a father who loved her, or the life her daughter would have known at Willow Bend. The sheriff had personally delivered the report confirming identification of the remains, but he couldn't definitively comment on local law enforcement's intentions regarding her mother. The county D.A. was reviewing the facts of the case, but it seemed doubtful charges would extend beyond concealment of a death or conspiracy. Try as she might, Randi couldn't yet summon any compassion for her mother. She'd given the police all the information she had, and it would be up to them to determine further action.

The mystery of Lavinia's shocking change of demeanor was solved by an internet search at the county library and a telephone conversation with an aunt Randi never knew she had. Her mother had lapsed into an accent that had a familiar inflection, and on a hunch, Randi had searched genealogical records of a half dozen counties in West Virginia. Lavinia had in fact been born and raised in poverty, and the stories Randi had been told of a privileged upbringing on the Eastern shore were nothing more than her mother's attempts to reinvent herself to fit her own idea of respectability. The truth was Lavinia had hitched a ride with a traveling salesman at the age of fourteen, ditching her widowed mother and younger siblings in favor of a one-way ticket out of town. Ironically, Randi had recognized the accent because Bill's relatives hailed from a town less than fifty miles from her mother's birthplace, a coincidence that explained her mother's refusal to get to know Bill or any of his kin. Lavinia's fear of being exposed as a charlatan was likely far more threatening to her than the secret she carried from Willow Bend, and Randi marveled again at the good health of a woman with so much to hide.

Randi willed Lavinia from her thoughts and set about the task at hand. She was expecting a very important visitor in a couple of days and she wanted everything to be ready.

CHAPTER TWENTY ONE

H enriette Benson proved to be a bright spot in the midst of it all. She'd been delighted to hear from Randi but was shocked to learn it was Henry Moore's daughter who now owned Willow Bend. She'd been sending letters every couple of years since 1995, in the hope that someone would reply. Henriette had flown down to Columbia within days of Randi's invitation, and the long drive to Willow Bend afforded her ample opportunity to fill in the rest of the story.

Henriette confirmed right away that Twig Williams was indeed her father. Henry Moore had befriended Lisette and her brothers many years ago, as he frequented her grandfather's club on Front Street. In those days, the music coming out of the black section of town was exciting and dangerous, qualities that were very alluring for white college boys just home for the summer. Lisette played piano in a band with her brothers, and Henry and his friends often hung out at the club despite the proprietor's suggestion that they keep to their own side of town. Despite the social mores of the day, Henry Moore had allowed his love of music and his interest in Lisette to override his common sense, and he'd slipped back to the club after his friends went home. Lisette was performing her final set when she saw Henry standing in the back motioning for her to come outside when she was done. He'd promised to bring her a record player and some recordings of new black artists, hoping to inspire her to move away and pursue a record deal. Henry had been impressed by Lisette and the boys, and he'd even offered to help them financially if they could escape their grandfather's controlling presence. That was the night they'd been caught out behind the club, and there had been hell to pay. Randi's father had been run off with a shotgun and the promise of death if he ever came back around. Lisette's punishment for consorting with a white man had been much harsher, and her younger brothers had watched in horror as their grandfather took a hot iron to the side of their sister's pretty face. As she screamed, he'd promised her that no man, black or white, would ever look at her again. From then on Lisette stayed hidden away in the house, swearing her brothers to secrecy regarding her disfigurement.

Some years later, one of the brothers summoned up the courage to seek out Henry Moore to advise him of Lisette's plight. With nowhere to go and a controlling grandfather who got meaner every day, there didn't seem to be much chance of a job, a life, or a future for Lisette. By then, Henry Moore had a wife and a baby daughter, but he felt responsible for the young woman's terrible fate. He vowed to do whatever he could to improve things for Lisette and arranged for her to move to a small house on Willow Bend. Sure, it was nothing but an old shack on a secluded farm, but at least she'd be able to go out and enjoy the sunshine and fresh air without fear of being seen. She'd made a living taking in washing and mending clothes for the other families, and for a time had worked in the main house as well. All of that had changed one fateful day when Mrs. Moore demanded that Lisette leave the house and never return. The birth of Lisette's baby had marked a turning point in relations, and Lavinia Moore had made no secret of her outrage and disdain for the mixed-race child. The mistress of Willow Bend had pronounced Lisette "too scary" to be around children and terminated the young woman's services despite her husband's objections. Randi had cringed to know her reaction to Lisette had led to the banishment, but she knew her mother well enough to know that one excuse was as good as another.

Randi and Hitch had accompanied Henriette to the old house, understanding she'd need some time to take it all in. Henriette had been about five at the time of their departure from Willow Bend, but her memories of the small house were strong and vivid. She went in every room and touched every object, sometimes smiling, and sometimes not. Randi had cleaned in anticipation of Henriette's arrival, even returning the photo and book to the mantle, just as she'd found it. Watching Lisette's daughter relive her early childhood memories was both touching and sobering. Randi had lost a father, and Lisette had lost a friend. Henry Moore had obviously cared for Henriette's mother, and his attempts to atone for the trouble he'd caused her continued over a period of years. Henriette knew her mother probably even loved Henry Moore, but instead had settled for the dubious attentions offered by Twig Williams in the absence of reciprocation.

The last days at Willow Bend for Henriette and Lisette were kicked off by a visit from Lavinia Moore, just days before her husband's disappearance hit the newspapers. Randi's mother entered the house carrying a large suitcase, suggesting that there would be unpleasant days ahead. It didn't take much convincing for Lisette to understand her privacy was in jeopardy, especially now that her benefactor was no longer around to shield her from the curious stares that were sure to come. Lisette had promptly sent a message to a sympathetic brother, enlisting his help for an escape from Willow Bend.

Henriette recalled they had waited until dark, taking only essential items and a lantern to guide them across the fields and down the road that led to town. Her Uncle Rueben had arranged for a truck to pick them up some distance from Willow Bend, and their new life had begun. The three of them had eventually made their way to New Jersey, and it was there Henriette had been raised in the meager comforts purchased by the money her mother took in for mending. Within a year, her uncle had secured a fine job with the railroad, and he and Lisette had reared Henriette in a happy home, even managing to send her to college. It was hard to imagine that Henriette's life would have been as good at Willow Bend, and Lavinia had likely done them a favor by forcing their exodus from South Carolina.

Henriette had promised to return with her husband and children the next time, and Randi had been happy to see the genuine fondness that seemed to be developing between Hitch and his half-sister. Just what Randi had to show for it all was a bit more ambiguous. Her mother's actions had absolutely changed the course of her life, but who could know if it would have been any better or worse? Some things weren't meant to be understood and allowing the past to color the future would only further the injustice. For all the looking back Randi had done these past few months, she was finally ready to look forward with hope. Lavinia's lies had surely set the stage for her daughter's past, but the future would be up to Randi.

EPILOGUE

T he evening is noisy, filled with the delightful sounds of frogs and crickets stirred up by a late Spring shower. Randi feels at peace in her rocking chair on the porch at Willow Bend, admiring the new paint and a freshly landscaped yard. Life is full now, and she can scarcely remember the woman she was when she first returned to this place. Looking back, she knows the journey was worth it. Coming to terms with the circumstances of her father's death had come only after the revelation of her mother's selfishness. She's moved beyond it now, focusing on tomorrow, the next day and the next. She knows what must be treasured is the present, and that the sweetest anticipations on this earth are the joys yet to be.

She reaches down to give Bo a good scratch behind the ears. He feels as at home here now as at the fish camp. Bo jerks his head to attention, listening intently for the sound of the truck coming down the lane. Randi laughs as he shakes her off and runs to meet his master. She can't blame him. She intends to give her husband a proper greeting too.

CPSIA information can be obtained
at www.ICGtesting.com
Printed in the USA
LVHW081300020420
652008LV00023B/3677